T0244716

BUTTER

ALSO BY GAYL JONES

FICTION

Corregidora (novel) (1975)
Eva's Man (novel) (1976)
White Rat (short stories) (1977)
The Healing (novel) (1998)
Mosquito (novel) (1999)
Palmares (novel) (2021)
The Birdcatcher (novel) (2022)

POETRY COLLECTIONS

Song for Anninho (1981)
The Hermit-Woman (1983)
Xarque and Other Poems (1985)
Song for Almeyda and Song for Anninho (2022)

OTHER WORKS

Chile Woman (play) (1974)
Liberating Voices: Oral Tradition in African American Literature (criticism) (1991)

BUTTER

NOVELLAS, STORIES, AND FRAGMENTS

GAYL JONES

Beacon Press
BOSTON

BEACON PRESS
Boston, Massachusetts
www.beacon.org

Beacon Press books
are published under the auspices of
the Unitarian Universalist Association of Congregations.

Printed in the United States of America

26 25 24 23 8 7 6 5 4 3 2 1

This book is printed on acid-free paper that meets the uncoated paper ANSI/NISO specifications for permanence as revised in 1992.

Text design and composition by Kim Arney

Excerpt from Don Steele's *Symbolism and Modernity* printed here by permission of the publisher.

Library of Congress Cataloging-in-Publication Data

Names: Jones, Gayl, author.
Title: Butter : novellas, stories, and fragments/ Gayl Jones.
Description: Boston : Beacon Press, [2023] | Summary: "A wide-ranging collection, including two novellas and ten stories exploring complex identities, from the acclaimed author of Corregidora, The Healing, and Palmares"—Provided by publisher.
Identifiers: LCCN 2022043207 (print) | LCCN 2022043208 (ebook) | ISBN 9780807030011 (cloth) | ISBN 9780807030028 (ebook)
Classification: LCC PS3560.O483 B87 2022 (print) | LCC PS3560.O483 (ebook) | DDC 813/.54—dc23/eng/20220913
LC record available at https://lccn.loc.gov/2022043207
LC ebook record available at https://lccn.loc.gov/2022043208

CONTENTS

BUTTER

A novella

I.

She buys one of those new Japanese-made, filmless cameras in order to photograph Remunda Eadweard. That's how Remunda spells her last name—Eadweard, not Edward. It's an ancient spelling of the name, perhaps going back to the time of Beowulf. A lot of modern people are spelling their last names like that again, returning to the original spelling from ancient or medieval times. It's very much in vogue. But as far as she knows, Remunda's family has always spelled its name that way.

But why does she spend so much time thinking about the name and about those years? First, it's important to know that Remunda Eadweard is her mother and that she met her for the first time in a café in London years ago. Or rather a pub, to be more exact. Remunda has thick, black hair and is not thoroughly English but a mixture of English, Welsh, Irish, Danish, and Swedish. Well, you can see her for yourself in the photograph her daughter Odelle has taken.

Once when Odelle was sitting in a Manhattan restaurant, before she met Remunda, she overheard two English women talking. She tried to picture Remunda as the woman they were referring to, though she'd see other people's pictures of

Remunda and knew the description didn't possibly fit. But every time she hears an English voice, she tries to imagine it's Remunda's, or someone who knows her. Anyway, this is what she overheard:

"She looks like an ordinary girl from Liverpool, if y'ask me. But she's the daughter of famous people, so everyone wants to photograph her. She looks like an ordinary girl to me, and her teeth are crooked."

She glanced about to see them thumbing through a copy of the French magazine *Elle*. They were eating marmalade on toast. One of the women was dabbing at crumbs with her forefinger. They were younger than they sounded, perhaps her age in those days. Thirtyish. One was petite with short, raisin-black hair. The other was a blonde. There was the smell of oranges and powdered sugar.

"I see her every day," said the other. "That same face, y'know. You see it everywhere and nobody's breaking down doors to get a picture of it."

"But I bet she enjoys knowing that, knowing that they wouldn't be at all interested in her for who she is. Don't y'think she enjoys knowing that?"

"She looks like any milkmaid, if y'ask me."

"We should go down to Miami and sit in the sun."

"I sunburn easily."

"I could live in the sun."

"It's just my forehead I've got to worry about. It peels."

"And I love the feel of water. I never swim. I tiptoe into the ocean."

"I can picture you at Brighton."

"I never go to Brighton, dear."

One of the women had a Fujica Auto Focus camera on the table.

She started to take pictures of her friend.

"Oh, no you don't," said the other one. "I'm not very photogenic. Everyone tells me how pretty I am, and then when you see me in a photo, I'm just not photogenic. Some gals who look great in pictures, you wouldn't even notice on the street."

Odelle took out her pen and jotted on the napkin a list of things she needed to buy: film, a new battery for the camera meter, PX13 and PX625 batteries, lens cleaner, lens cleaning tissues, lens brush, 100% rag paper for mounting prints, Vivitar Bigmouth Developing Tank trays, color print drums, Omega analyzer, exposure computer. One needed all of that paraphernalia then.

In the booth across from her, a man was eating pizza and the woman with him, noodles with bits of seafood. The woman kept loading noodles on her fork and hogging it down. The man nibbled.

But for a long time, Odelle had stopped photographing people and took up photographing things. It became an obsession, a compulsion. She photographed everything: the corners of rooms, a pink radiator, a carpet stain, Scotch tape, butter. She was really banalyzing the art. Still, they put some of the photos in a museum, and she labeled the show *Private Subjectivism* and she actually had buyers. So she continued taking photographs of such inconsequentialities; that people actually bought them made her shrug and wonder. The gallery director praised them; she talked about how such photographs looked easier to take than they actually were. It's harder than it looks to take a really good photograph, she said. And what did Odelle think? Which ones were her favorites? Odelle answered that her favorite pictures were the ones she hadn't intended, those she didn't realize she'd taken until after she'd developed the photo. The gallery director said that wasn't exactly what she meant.

It was Dante who suggested that she go and visit Remunda. Or rather who was the catalyst for what she always wanted to do anyway. But needed the push or nerve. She remembered it like she remembers everything, as a continuing present, even those old days: she is photographing Dante, her boyfriend, the musician and composer, who is sitting at his piano. She photographs him first and then the sheets of composer's paper piled on top of the piano. Music manuscript paper, he calls it. It's a thin paper he orders especially from a company in Youngstown, Ohio, because it has multiple staves. He always orders the twelve-stave, deluxe pad. But she can't remember why it's better than any other music manuscript paper. And he has a blueprint machine. What does a musician need with a blueprint machine? And he keeps a list of other places where the multiple-stave paper can be gotten; it can be gotten at Educator's Music in Cleveland, Harris Teller's in Chicago, Volkwein's Music in Pittsburg. And the first time he asked her, "Have you seen my master?" she didn't know what in the hell he meant. "Master," he repeated. "You know." No, she didn't know. He went about and found it himself. Made her feel stupid that she didn't know. When anyone said "master," the only thing she could think of was slavery, not music. Then he played the piece. She'd gone out onto the terrace, but it traveled to her, changing as it came. It sneaked up on her and nudged her shoulder and said, "I'm what you like." She tried to stay indifferent to it, but it made her dance. Standing against the music, she rested her chin on its shoulder. She interlaced her fingers with its fingers. The music got closer and whispered something.

She couldn't quite hear it. But then there was Dante standing there at the glass doors, watching her. He came out onto the terrace, and she held her head up simply, and they kissed.

"Need something to distract me," she says.

"What?"

She says it again.

"I don't mean to bore you with my problem," she says.

"Sure you mean to."

She tries to remember the guy who advised his son never to entertain other people with his personal problems and private affairs. "Though they're interesting to you," he said. "They're tedious and impertinent to everyone else."

She's had a string of boyfriends, real ones and dream ones: an electrician, a plumber, a high school football coach, a motorcycle repairman, a welder in an automobile plant, a diver, a coast guardsman, a gardener, an organizer of socialist cooperatives, mostly rough-and-ready types. She didn't know how the organizer sneaked in there. Was he the sort who'd please Remunda? Dante was born in Nassau in the Bahamas and composes contemporary music that has its base in the music of Junkanoo.

She photographs the piano keys. She photographs Dante reaching up and scratching notes on composer's paper. She photographs a "master." She photographs some sheet music. She lights up one of the Chesterfields they keep for houseguests.

"Leave me some peace, just for a minute," he mumbles.

She goes into the kitchen and photographs condiments. Salt, pepper, garlic powder, onion powder, cinnamon. She returns to the living room, grabs a handful of Chesterfields, then goes into the darkroom. She leans against the darkroom wall and smokes one cigarette, one after another.

After a while, Dante comes to the darkroom door and knocks. "You okay in there?" he asks.

"Yeah, sure."

"Come on, let's go to dinner."

She exits with a handful of cigarette butts.

"You smoke all o' that crap?" he asks. "That's the worst crap in the wul for ya."

"Then how come we keep 'em for the guests?" she asks.

"Their choice," he says.

In the kitchen she dumps the butts into the trash compactor.

She thinks of her last showing of photographs—the one of inconsequentialities.

What do you feel taking pictures? An interviewer had asked her once.

What do you mean what do I feel? she'd asked.

I mean does it make you feel well, I don't know. Safe or in danger?

I just feel.

Well, what do you mean by feel?

She didn't answer.

But do you think that the photographs are truly worthy of our attention, I mean, that photograph of butter, for example? And aren't you Remunda Eadweard's daughter?

Remunda . . . How'd you know about Remunda?

She sits back in one of the straight-back chairs along the wall while the interviewer rattles off her biography: A war baby, born in London. Her father, an Afro-American—do you prefer Black or Afro-American?—soldier stationed in London. They met in a bomb shelter during the Blitz. Very romantic, etc. Her father brought her back to America when she was still a baby. How come? But that's not the usual war-baby story, is it? I mean, don't most GIs just leave the kid? Korea, Vietnam, and all? . . .

She says nothing. Remunda's a photographic journalist and art photographer who takes real photographs—the Biafran War, Guinea Bissau; or real landscapes—Futa Jallon highlands or those of Southern Algeria; or real people—brick makers in Guyana or Sotho potters; or exotic animals—the oribi. No common zebras for Remunda. In fact, she has a signed book of photographs—signed from Remunda, with love. What does a camera feel? Next to Remunda's photographs, hers seem the most inconsequential in the world.

"Lock up your camera, take a holiday, why don't you?" Dante had asked back then. "Maybe you should go visit Remunda, why don't you?"

Lock up your cameras? Imagine that? Imagine telling him to lock up his piano? Or his keyboard? Or his music?

And in fact, when he said that, she looked at him in wonder, not because of the prate about locking up her cameras, but that he even knew who Remunda was. She'd forgotten ever having told him about Remunda. Well, at least naming her. He persisted with the bit about locking the cameras up, and then he said, "Go to London. Maybe you'll come back and take better pictures."

"My pictures ain't half bad," she mumbled.

"Recharge," he said.

As they walk down the street toward the restaurant, she looks at their reflections superimposed over objects in the glass windows: wine glasses, a VCR, candelabra, sweatshirts. "Palimpsest" pops into her head. Palimpsest, though, has to do with words, doesn't it, not images. It always surprises her that her reflection is so fair and Dante's, so dark. She doesn't feel her color. She feels darker. She read somewhere that Robert Redford had said he didn't feel blond; he felt like a brunet; he felt dark. She feels like a darker woman. Up North sometimes, too, they mistake her for a white woman. Only in the South do they seem to know she's Black. Or Afro-American.

Someone behind them with a radio passes. She hears snippets of Joe Cocker's "I'm a Civilized Man." "You're lucky I'm a civilized man," he sings to a woman who'd done 'im wrong. You're lucky I'm a civilized woman, she thinks, though Dante hasn't actually done 'er wrong. What could she say of him? Sometimes it seems like he's on one planet and she's on another. Sometimes she travels to his to meet him; other times she invites him to hers. He surveys her planet, explores it, discovers things, but always goes back to his own.

Shouldn't lovers journey to a new world, neither one's nor the other's? Once, looking out at the ocean, Dante said, "That ocean's a perfect blue." But it wasn't blue at all to her; it was green. He swam and bathed in the sun, and she roamed about taking pictures of lovers, triple exposed. As she photographed, she kept trying to remember what it was Flaubert had said about passion. She'd written a paper on it for a Comparative Literature class in college, a whole paper, and she couldn't remember now what it was at all. They had read La Rochefoucauld and Rousseau, but nobody Black, nobody African, in those days, and one Asian woman whose name she couldn't remember, Lady something. She'd wanted to write her paper on Achebe or Tutuola, but she'd chickened out and done someone safe: Flaubert. Nothing magnifies passion like art? Was that it? The lovers whose pictures she took seemed like such small souls, embracing, but when she blew their pictures up . . . Well, nothing magnifies passion like art. But did she dare call it art? *Quincunx* she called that series of five lovers, triple exposed.

"Hungry?" he asks.

"Some," she replies.

"Let's grab a bite t'eat in here," he says.

She thinks he means Horn and Hardart's, but he's glanced toward the right.

"Okay," she says. "Was that lyricist really named Glasscock, the one who sent you those lyrics?"

It's redundant, but she feels redundant sometimes. Lyricists are always sending him lyrics.

"Naw, the song was called 'Glasscock Island.' Maybe change it to 'Glass Island.' Now that would be a title."

"You darn right."

Pushing in glass doors, they touch their own reflections. Inside, stranger, latent images. Dante directs her away from the crowd toward a corner table. In the background, a woman's tender, idle comment. Odelle orders a salad. Dante, a steak with mushrooms.

"Is it a real island?" she asks.

"Naw, I think it's supposed to be a symbol."

"Rather blatant, ain't it? And perverse."

Eating mushrooms, Dante only nods. Salad stuck in her jaws, Odelle smiles.

"The lyricist must be a woman," she says, after a moment.

"How'd you guess?"

"I couldn't imagine a man calling a song Glasscock anything, only a woman."

"Oh, yeah?"

Dante shoves some of his mushrooms onto her plate. She puts bits of salad onto his. She nibbles the mushrooms, which are garlic-flavored. Her favorite flavoring. In the background, two women jabber; they complain of small, picky things. She wonders if they were not two women but two men talking of the same matter, whether she'd consider the things small and picky or of consequence. No. Still small and picky. She nibbles mushrooms and wonders how they'd look in photographs—the mushrooms, not the women.

She and Dante are not talking and so she is thinking of a volume of contemporary American poetry Dante gave her. It surprised her a bit, Dante giving her a volume of poetry, but Dante said he always read poetry for musical inspiration. All kinds of poetry. And she read and reread James Dickey's "Power and Light." It made her think of Ralph Ellison, though, not James Dickey. She wondered what it would have been like if Ellison's Invisible Man had spoken on his lower frequencies, not from underground but climbing the poles and towers of the power and light company. Even reading poetry makes her see things she'd like to photograph: "barrel-cracks of plaster . . . the seal on the bottle . . . heads of nails . . . wires . . . limed rafters . . . dice dots . . . watch . . . gloves . . . shoes . . . a double handful of wires . . . sparklers . . . a limp piece of bread . . . a bulb . . ." Her favorite poem in the contemporary American poetry book was Gary Snyder's "Riprap." Dante has two favorites: Robert Lowell's "Man and Wife" and Gwendolyn Brooks's "Boy Breaking Glass." At first she misread a line in the glass poem as "The music is in minors." But her favorite line was "The only sanity is a cup of tea." She tried to photograph it, the cup of tea, but the photograph stayed merely a cup of tea and nothing more than that, nothing magical and other. And Imamu Amiri Baraka's "Three Modes of History and Culture" gave her things to photograph too: "chalk mark . . . telephones . . . windows . . . milk . . . cardboard trunks . . ." "All talk is energy," said Baraka. She liked to skim through the poems, building a collage of words and rhythms; said: enough sense loves beautiful shoes bluegreen doorframe the mirror meanwhile jiggle the contraption of your hidden equator.

And she would quote from John Ashbery's "Self-Portrait in a Convex Mirror" and called Dante for a while "Francesco": "Your argument, Francesco," she would say, "has begun to grow stale." "What argument?" he'd ask. He looked at her like she was a weirdo. But no answer or answers were forthcoming.

Really, she feels it is not objects that she wants to photograph but ambiguities. Dante asks what ambiguities can be found in a cup of tea.

Now, she looks across the table at Dante with his sleeves rolled up. His upper arms are still muscular and tight from all the years of working in his father's construction company. He refused to play the boss's boy, in the office behind a desk, but laid bricks and carried beams and whatever construction workers carried. Would James Dickey call such work "I Am a Man" work? She wonders. And surely Dante climbed poles and towers, though he worked for his father and not the Bahamian Light and Power Company. (She wondered if there was a light and power company in Ellison's book; she tried to remember.) But that made him more attractive to her, that he was both cerebral and muscular, athletic and aesthetic. She wants to reach over and touch the muscles in his upper arms, but she doesn't. She thinks of Robert Creeley's "Cat Bird Singing." Catbird, catbird.

She has never been tempted to photograph catbirds.

Dante can compose anything: rock, rhythm and blues, funk, soul, new wave, jazz, blues, classical, country, reggae, rap, Junkanoo. He prides himself on being cosmopolitan, of combining many different types of music, in a sort of musical fusion sometimes, even though Junkanoo is his base. He likes it that critics have not been able to pinpoint a Dante song. He prides himself on having a multifarious style. He's even written Broadway show tunes.

Odelle pretends to be ignorant of music. She pretends not to know the difference between sforzando and allargando. But Dante edited a musical dictionary. She knows the terms, but she can't hear them. She has a tin ear, or so she says she does, and can carry a tune only in a bucket. The only music she listens to, besides Dante's, is music that Dante calls vapid and sentimental. But for Dante, music is not just music. Now he's working on a book on music theory, focusing on music in Africa and the African diaspora. He doesn't see music as merely entertainment; entertainment's only surface; it has a deeper more complex meaning. In the Junkanoo Festival, for instance, most tourists only saw and heard the entertainment but not the other dimensions. She's read passages of his manuscript, but she doesn't fully understand the difference between music's deep structure and its surface structure. She gets tangled in the talk of melody and chords and harmonics and its relationship to culture and language and human values. But she thinks he's onto something.

She says, "You're onto something." But he doesn't just listen to African and African diaspora music. When he can't sleep, he listens to Bach's *Goldberg Variations*. At least, she thinks it's called *Goldberg Variations*. Dante said that Bach wrote it for a friend of his who was an insomniac. When she said most of the classical musicians must have had friends who were insomniacs, he didn't think it was very funny. He didn't get the joke. He gave her a lesson in Mozart and Wagner and Berlioz and Vivaldi. Of Mozart, he played for her one of the keyboard pieces Mozart had written at age five, and he made her listen to *The Marriage of Figaro* and *The Magic Flute*, which he called *Zauberflote*, interrupting the music as he lectured, or rather interrupting his lectures with pieces of the operas. So, she didn't joke about music anymore.

"Almost time for *La Dolce Vita*," she says.

"What?"

"*La Dolce Vita*."

"Yeah, sure."

She'd said she wanted to get back from dinner in time to see *La Dolce Vita*. Dante finishes his mushrooms. She gulps her wine. He calls for the bill, pays the check. He tells her she's silly. What does she think they've got a VCR for? But she can never time them right.

Back at the apartment, they sit together on the sofa, Dante's arm around her shoulder. She doesn't know how many times she's seen this movie. Marcello Mastroianni, Anita Ekberg, Anouk Aimee, Yvonne Furneaux. Rubini, Sylvia, Maddalena, Emma . . . Italian movies, says Dante, are like wandering rocks. He loves Fellini too. But he doesn't feel like Fellini has progressed. He feels like Fellini keeps doing the same movie. "But what a movie. The best movie in the world." It's like the jazz musician he once told her about. This bunch of jazz musicians were having a jam session and another of them sits in on it; they're improvising a song; this jazz musician who sits in on it plays maybe for an hour with them, then he has to leave. He leaves, takes care of some business, and then, maybe three hours later, he comes back—and they're still playing the same song!

Well, Dante can tell it better than she can remember it. After *La Dolce Vita*, they watch another Italian movie. You know the one. With Sophia Loren. Odelle's favorite scene is the one in the kitchen when Sophia's husband picks up the hem of her dress and wipes his hands on it. It's not exactly her favorite scene, but it's the one that sticks with her. She's seen that scene almost as many times as she's seen *La Dolce Vita*. It's funny how it sticks with her, but Dante hardly remembers it at all. It's just a little scene, but for her it somehow explains the whole movie. Dante scarcely remembers it. The scene that sticks with Dante is the one where Sophia and her lover, played by Marcello Mastroianni, are searching for something to say to each other. For Dante, that's the scene that tells everything.

"See it," she says.

"What?"

"Wiping the hands on her dress."

"Yeah, what?"

She reaches for a Chesterfield and lights up.

"At it again?" he asks as she inhales.

She flicks ash into a tray.

"Tell me what you mean," he says.

"Sophia's really beautiful, isn't she?" she says.

He says something about Sophia being beyond beauty, about Sophia being somewhere in the stratosphere.

She puffs until his scene comes up, then she puts the cigarette in the tray, like a dropped conversation. She gives a lazy, idle stare toward the screen, as Sophia and Marcello search for something to say to each other.

She wonders what it would be like to be so beautiful you were beyond beauty. Dante wipes ash from her skirt. Watching an Italian movie, you feel as if you've wandered somewhere. Could he also mean that? Drowsy, she lights another cigarette. She wonders why the scenes that men love and remember are not the same ones women do. But Dante's not every man, and she's not every woman. She looks toward him.

"Don't give me that lost gaze," he says.

His eyebrows hook. He turns back toward the screen, toward Sophia. She falls asleep and dreams that she's in an Italian movie. There are a maze of hallways and rooms.

There is no music in her dream. (She wonders if Dante's dreams are song-filled?) When she wakes up, Dante's brushing more ash from her blue denim skirt.

"Didn't smoking used to upset your stomach?" he asks.

She nods but pulls the ashtray near and lights up another cigarette, inhaling.

"What're you watching?" she asks.

"Some new show."

Another kitchen scene. In this one, a young man is sitting in a kitchen chair; a young blonde woman straddles him; they're kissing.

"Do you want a Pepsi Cola?" she asks.

Not the woman on the TV screen, but Odelle.

"Yeah, thanks."

She gets up, goes into the kitchen, and comes back with two Pepsis.

She gives him his and sets hers on the end table. On the TV screen a woman with a high-pitched voice is talking about birds. But she herself is thinking of the ocean. Someone said women didn't like the ocean, but she can't remember who just now. She's photographed oceans. Remunda's photographed them, too, but more exotic oceans, or rather, the view of oceans from more exotic places. Odelle has photographed more soap than oceans. More lettuce.

She even tried to photograph a cat's meow.

Dante squeezes her shoulder. She watches the man and woman in the kitchen. They've never made love in the kitchen, her and Dante. Now he's kissing the tip of her ear—Dante, not the man on TV. Then he goes to the piano, a blond piano. He tinkles it.

Then he makes a deeper music, a deeper, African sound. Why does she think "African sound"? Why can't the lighter sound be African music too? One of the poets said a kiss was a bird. If she photographed a bird, would that be the same as photographing a kiss? The interviewer asked her what her hobbies were: reading poetry and watching TV. And movies. If a kiss is a bird, then what is a bird's kiss?

Dante, at the piano, plays all the keys. He keeps changing the rhythm. How he makes love, she's thinking. Keeps changing the rhythm. Once she's learned one rhythm and she's moving with him, he shifts to another, and she must relearn. Dah, dah-dah, dah-dah-dah-dah. He moves behind a beat, then above it, then beyond it. He never moves with a rhythm she could mistake for her own.

Going into the bedroom, she puts on her nightshirt, a long purple one with an embroidered pocket; she brushes her dark brown hair, the sort they used to call "good hair" in the old days. She thinks of Sophia Loren again. She tries to remember all of the Sophia Loren movies she's seen. She thinks of *Two Women*. She thinks of *Marriage Italian Style*. She turns on the radio, soft, sentimental music. She thinks of Dante wiping his dirty hands on the hem of her nightshirt. Perhaps Sophia's dress was already dirty (from working in the kitchen) and the man thought, *Well, what's the difference? Kids tugging at her skirt all day.* In the basement of her father's house in Connecticut, there is a punching bag, a rowing machine, and bicycles. She thinks of Sophia, at the end of the day, going into the basement and making use of the punching bag. Then she thinks of Sophia again, this time punching Marcello, or rather trying to. It's one of those Laurel and Hardy scenes, the one where you're punching at someone and they've got their arms held out, holding your head, and their arms are so long and yours so short that instead of punching them, you're punching the air. So, that's what Sophia's doing, punching the air. She wonders whether it would be one of Sophia's comedies or dramas.

"Come in and hear this," shouts Dante.

She returns to the living room and sits on the couch, but she can't hear the music for thoughts of Dante's sister.

"Why do you go about calling yourself Black?" she'd asked.

Melda's her name.

"Because I am," Odelle had answered.

Melda said America bewildered her. All the Europeans going about calling themselves Black. Even dark-toned mulattoes from America she'd point to, asking Odelle, "Are they Black?" and Odelle would answer, "Yes."

All through Manhattan she'd tug Odelle's sleeve. "And that one?"

"Yes."

"What about that one?"

"No, he's Puerto Rican."

"How can you tell?"

Odelle said she just could. She didn't know how. She just could. She didn't tell Melda that she herself had been mistaken more than once for nearly everything. Except, she kept reminding herself, in the South. The best racial detectives seemed to be southerners.

She supposed they had to be, because of the history.

She drove up with Odelle to Providence, to the Rhode Island School of Design, where Odelle had been invited to lecture on photography. (What do you think of Sontag? was the only question she remembered.)

"Are they Black?"

"No, they're Portuguese."

It made her even more bewildered. She brooded over it. It amazed her. She brooded over Odelle too. And you, you consider yourself Black? Of course, replied Odelle. She thought of the one-drop rule, the one-drop theory. When she had gone to see Remunda in London, she'd left London and spent a few weeks in Spain, photographing castles. She met a woman there whom she offended by talking about the woman's African ancestry. You could see Africa in the woman, but the woman refused it. Even as a remote ancestral possibility. She assured Odelle—naming her father, a respected merchant, an old family, *un hombre superior*—she assured Odelle that she was "pure white." Africa peeped out everywhere.

One hidden equator. But she was pure white. Perhaps Odelle should have said Moors, not Africans. The Moors who were in Spain for . . . was it centuries? "Tus antepasados moros, de sangre puro."

My father is Don So-and-So, the woman insisted, and we are Old Christians. His name rolled off the young woman's tongue like butter, but Odelle couldn't remember it. It was an elegant-sounding name, and the woman said it sacredly. Don Arellano?

She thought of her as she and Melda walked down Prospect Street in Providence and she pointed out the Portuguese. Black? No, Portuguese. They went to a pizza parlor and Melda kept giving her that brooding look. Again, a tug on the sleeve and a question.

She nodded toward a tall, ginger-colored man. "Portuguese?"

"No, Black."

"But how can you tell? How can you tell the difference?"

It was funny actually. She smiled and the man must have thought she was smiling at him, because he smiled back. She didn't tell Melda that she could see, besides Africa, Ireland in his features and Native America, maybe Cherokee or Cree or even Navajo or Kiowa, and even Mexican all mixed in together. She recognized him, suddenly, thought she knew him. Wasn't he one of the poets in one of Dante's poetry books?

She took out a picture of her father and showed Melda. Her father was as dark as Melda and Dante. Melda's mouth dropped open. Then she had no photograph of Remunda. She merely explained her.

"In the Bahamas . . . Jamaica . . . the Caribbean . . . you'd be . . ."

Was she going to say white? Or was the preferred term "biracial"? She tried to remember what she had read about race and ethnicity in the Caribbean.

Originally, Melda and Dante's family was from Jamaica, she explained. Still, it was hard for her to understand how Odelle had chosen Dante over, say, one like that one, and she nodded toward the ginger-colored man. The poet?

Odelle said nothing, and Melda laughed, a high-pitched laugh.

When Dante went to bed, she stayed up and watched another movie, an old one with Ray Milland, Marjorie Reynolds, and Carl Esmond.

"I know I sound insane," one of the characters said. "You are, without a doubt," replied the other.

It had the atmosphere of a Hitchcock movie, but it wasn't a Hitchcock movie. She wondered whether if Hitchcock had directed it, whether it would be considered a classic now. Then she switched the channel. A woman on the screen was laughing. Bursts of laughter, ricocheting laughter. She'd missed the joke. She switched to another channel, a rebroadcast of an ice-skating championship.

"Her name and her look would lead you to think she's of Asiatic origin, but she's an American," says the announcer.

Odelle watches the skater do a sort of twirling jump. "Ah, a flaw," says one announcer.

"Ah, just a little flaw," rejoins the other.

Odelle herself hasn't seen any flaw, but she isn't a skater. She turns the channel back to Ray Milland. When finally she goes into the bedroom, Dante is already asleep. When she sleeps, she dreams that she and Dante are standing at a seawall. Dante resembles Ray Milland. Dante keeps looking out to sea and she keeps watching him, hoping that he'll come to resemble himself again. She pulls out a pack of cigarettes from the pocket of her sweater-vest, pulls out two cigarettes, puts them both in her mouth, lights them, then gives one to him. She thinks he's going to protest that he doesn't smoke, but he doesn't, he takes it, puffs, then looks seaward again. Where do all your romantic ideas come from? he asks her. The movies? Instead of answering, she puffs and puffs and puffs and puffs. Someone who resembles an Aborigine—Dante refers to them as Native Australians—or bushman walks along the wall, balancing himself. The acrobat takes her attention away from Dante. She watches the acrobat, but Dante keeps looking seaward. When the man gets to where Dante and she are standing, he pauses in front of them and gives them a lecture on Captain Cook, the English explorer and navigator. "Okeh?" he asks when he finishes the lecture. "Okeh," she answers. But Dante keeps watching the sea. It's Dante who had told her about lucid dreams, the sort of dreams you have where you know you're dreaming, the kind you're supposed to try to learn from.

"In lucid dreaming, you know you're in a dream . . . You can even wake up inside the dream, like you'd wake up inside a movie . . ."

At breakfast, Dante asks her what the movie was about. "Kermesse," she says.

He says nothing. He merely butters toast. Then he asks, "What in the hell is Kermesse?"

2.

Odelle had met Dante in the Bahamas. Nassau, on Providence Island. She had gone there for a photographer's convention but became too preoccupied with the beauty of the place to spend time in the convention hotel. She'd rented a car and driven along the stretches of roadway, trying to remember that here in the Bahamas one drove on the left not the right. It was the same as in England.

And the roadways were immaculate. Palm trees grew alongside the road. There were few automobiles in the direction that she'd taken, away from the popular beaches. Here, in this place, she felt there was the most beauty she'd seen. She felt as though she belonged here. She turned down a road leading to a beach. (All the roads seemed to lead to beaches.) This was not a beach exactly but a sort of cove. She thought it was deserted till she saw a man, barefoot, wearing khaki shorts, no shirt, and sitting on a rock. He held a bag of sponges. She had asked if she could photograph him. They had started talking. About the sponges mostly. About how only native Bahamians could dive for sponges or coral or any of the island's resources; foreigners were forbidden to. At first, she learned later, he had thought she was Canadian and white, but then there was something that she'd said, some fleeting comment, some turn of phrase, some expression or attitude that made him realize that she was an African American.

And there was something he said too, some turn of phrase that made her realize that he was not just a diver for sponges to sell in the marketplace for tourists. She mentioned that she'd always wanted to learn to scuba dive—"for underwater photography, you know"—and he said he'd teach her. She photographed the scuba gear on the sand at his feet, then she said she hadn't planned to be in the Bahamas long enough to learn that, but he said something about teaching her the rudiments in a few lessons. Also, he had some oceanographer friends who'd invited him to go diving with them. (He'd said "oceanographer people," and he hadn't told her it was his boat they'd rented or, rather, his father's, who had not only a construction company but a boat-rental company as well.)

When she left him (promising to meet him the next day to learn the "rudiments") she went to the nearest camera store and bought a Nikon underwater camera. The next day she met him at the cove.

No, no, he'd said about her taking the camera down right off; she'd have to wait a bit for underwater pictures. But by the time they were to go diving with the oceanographer people, she was ready, her camera loaded.

The oceanographer people were all Scandinavians. She'd expected Bahamians. (She'd called them "Norwegians"—all Scandinavians looked the same to her.) They seemed like aliens from another world. The leader of the group, a specialist in marine vegetation, who'd written articles on farming the oceans of the world, was named Dr. Jomfruen I. Ulveham; her friends, however, called her Jomfrey. Others on the boat were Dr. Varulven, Dr. Bosmer, Dr. Eyvind, and another woman, Dr. Gerd Jytte. Dante, of course, didn't call them Doctor anything. They were Jomfrey, Guri, Aagot, Aurand, Gudrun, Gerd, etc. She couldn't remember any of the names except for Jomfrey and Gerd, who, instead of talking about oceanography were on the deck raving about a new shampoo with Protena-9, some sort of natural curl energizer that made the hair curl up without being permed. They were fascinated by how her hair stayed curly underwater. They were both from Denmark; Gerd's father was a kaolin miner. Kaolin, she explained, was used to make porcelain. Jomfrey was from a family of fishermen and shipbuilders. They stood around her on deck running their fingers through her curly hair until it was time to get together their scuba gear. They were to be collecting and labeling specimens of marine plants. Of course none of the specimens could be taken out of the Bahamas, Jomfrey said; they would be given to a local marine museum or tossed back into the ocean.

Odelle swam between Dante and Jomfrey while the others swam ahead. She wondered if Dante and Jomfrey were more than friends as they swam near underwater caves and entered one.

Inside they swam up up up up until they reached the surface inside the cave. She photographed while Jomfrey climbed out of the water to put bits of green vegetation into her sack. Odelle wondered how these, growing in the cave, could still be termed "marine vegetation." Then they dove down again, and she photographed not the fish or underwater plants but rock formations, shaped by water, that seemed like human carvings. Then she saw some seaweed and reached to pull at it (it was in the way of one of the rock formations), and it reached back at her and seized her wrist. The others laughed, and Dante freed her, pulling apart the colorful, jeweled leaves.

She thought it was like one of those land plants that trap flies and insects—the Venus flytrap, for example—but later, on board ship, Dante explained that it wasn't a plant—not seaweed—but a water animal that had evolved that way for chameleon—no—camouflage purposes. Then one of the rocks she was photographing turned out to be a sort of fish. Another camouflage effect. Rock separating from rock and swimming toward her.

They entered another underwater cave, this one well lit from some invisible source of light above them. She and Dante climbed up onto the bank, but the others continued swimming, gathering their specimens. It was there that he kissed her. And they dove under water again. Then Jomfrey was looking at her in a way that looked dangerous behind her mask. Yes, he and Jomfrey had probably been lovers. (Dante swore they'd never been.)

As she swam near Jomfrey, Jomfrey swam faster. Then on deck, Jomfrey began calling the names of the plants they'd gathered, plants she said flourished only under water. (She was working on a book called *Marine Plants in the Bahamas*.)

"These look like mushrooms," Odelle commented. "They thrive only under water," Jomfrey repeated. "Yes," echoed Gerd. "Only under water."

It was a fascinating assortment of marine plants, all colors, shapes, and sizes, but they were prevented from taking any out of the country, Jomfrey repeated. They did, however, let Odelle photograph everything.

Jomfrey, whom she learned was from an island in Denmark called Laaland, asked her why she hadn't photographed any fish.

"The fish in those caves are used to having their pictures taken," she said. "Some of them even have names. That 'rock' that swam toward you, that's Geronimo . . . Lend me your camera."

When Odelle gave her the camera, she snapped Odelle's picture.

"Send me one," she said, and gave Odelle an address in Laaland.

Then she told Odelle about the Blue Grotto in Capri, Italy, all full of brilliant blue light. One comes to it, like the caves here, from the sea, she explained. Talking, her eyes, too, were full of brilliant blue light.

After the oceanographic expedition, Odelle went back with Dante to his cottage. He fixed her hot chocolate with cinnamon. He'd sold a few of his songs to a publisher in Montreal and now wanted to devote himself full time to composition. He'd saved a little money to tide him over for a while, he said. She sipped the hot chocolate with cinnamon and listened to him play a song on his keyboard. She thought he'd kiss her again, but he didn't. He played the keyboard, one song after another. After listening to the first few songs, she wandered into his bathroom, took a bath, and washed her hair. He had Galenic bath oil *pour les peaux sensibles* and some sort of organic, hypoallergenic shampoo.

When she came back to the front room, he was watching television. He turned toward her and smiled slightly and patted the seat beside him. She sat down on the couch. He was watching a television movie based on a story by Gabriel Garcia Márquez about the smell of roses coming from the sea. It took place in a seacoast village. Suddenly the villagers started smelling roses that came in from the sea.

She was half watching the movie and half waiting for him to kiss her again as he'd done in the underwater cave. She remembered that a woman had once told her that women didn't like the sea. She'd taught a photography class at a small girls' school and then with her salary had rented a house on the New England coast, one of those ragged, rocky coasts without a beach. She had photographed the seawall and was standing at the seawall photographing the ocean when a woman came up to her, a tall, angular, gray-haired woman with a hawk's beak nose. The woman's hair was long and tied back with a rubber band. She had perfect cheekbones, high, the skin along them tight. She wore a plaid shirt and khaki trousers. Odelle imagined her as a writer or artist, but never asked. Perhaps she was neither. Perhaps she was a fisherman's wife.

Odelle did not stop photographing as the woman talked. Her camera raised, she photographed the sea and rocky coast and the sudden flash of seagulls. As she photographed, the woman talked, like background music. She was thinking of the sea and that woman talking as Dante reached toward her and unbuttoned her blouse and the belt of her slacks.

The sea, the woman said, was what men tested their manhood by. Men who live by the sea and who go to sea.

Except for her perfect cheekbones, the rest of her features were as jagged and angular as the coastline.

And what of women? she'd asked.

The woman had frowned and said nothing.

Then she said the thing about women not liking the ocean, and she walked back up the coast, picking her way along rock. Odelle watched her through the camera lens but didn't photograph her.

Instead she turned back to photograph the sea.

Some woman from a photography magazine had planned to drive up and interview her that day, but she'd been intimidated by the coastline. So, she telephoned.

What are you trying to capture in your photographs? she asked.

Something like what Jung said, Odelle answered. About how experience comes to us in fragments.

The woman made cooing noises and sounded impressed.

Odelle could picture the woman's eyes brightening as she jotted it down. Really, she hadn't been trying to capture anything of the kind; she'd just been trying to get . . . She didn't know what she'd been trying to get.

A question Melda had asked her popped into her head. "Would you like to get Blacker?" Melda had asked. No, she'd asked, "Do you wish you were Blacker?" She'd nodded.

Then the interviewer asked her about the "self-portrait photograph of herself" (that's how the woman expressed it) where she's holding the camera up in front of her, like a mask.

I hear you're by nature camera shy? she asked. Yes.

Isn't that odd? A photographer who's camera shy. What would you like to do if you weren't a photographer?

Uh, work theater lights.

Now that's done electronically, you know. Yes, I know.

Then the woman started mentioning the Sabattier effect and Mackie lines. Odelle couldn't remember what those were, but Yes seemed an appropriate answer, so she answered, Yes.

I love the way you've begun to reduce the world to, say, a screw, or a spool of thread . . .

(Had she done that? Even in those days? She tried to remember something Gwendolyn Brooks said about spaces.)

What are you photographing now? the woman asked. Ocean. Seacoast.

The woman didn't coo, but she scribbled something, and then thanked her.

Dante whispered something against her ear. Yes, she answered.

Afterwards, he made her more hot chocolate with cinnamon.

They ate honey-coated donuts and fruit cups filled with chunky melons and pineapples.

3.

She arrives at the airport in London and takes a taxi to the Royal Garden Hotel. She'd first booked at the Eden, but a friend of Dante's had told her that the Royal Garden was at the edge of the Kensington Gardens, and she remembered reading a Virginia Woolf story that took place there. So she'd changed to the Royal Garden.

After she tips the porter, she stands at the window, smoking a Phillip Morris and staring down into the Kensington Gardens, or what she believes is it. Hyde Park, she'd been told, was also nearby, as well as Knightsbridge and Piccadilly. She'd heard of Piccadilly but not of Knightsbridge. Dante's friend had been an exchange student in London and had given her all sorts of telephone numbers of friends and friends of friends, but she doesn't dare use them. She's nervous enough at meeting Remunda for the first time. So nervous in fact that she hasn't written or telephoned that she's coming to London.

She finishes the cigarette and stares at the tentacles of the color TV. Then she turns it on.

She sits on the edge of the bed and leans forward with her elbows on her knees. She feels like a mudfish. (She doesn't know what a mudfish is, but she'd heard Dante's sister Melda once talk about feeling like a mudfish.) She doesn't open her suitcase. It stays in the corner of the hotel room where the porter had set it.

It doesn't have a camera in it. Dante had said, "Leave it here," and so she stupidly had. Now she'd like to photograph something—maybe the open Phillip Morris package. Or maybe the suitcase or the walls. She knows a photographer who photographed nothing but walls, all kinds of walls; but his walls were more interesting than these walls. She doesn't know him; she knows his photographs merely. She has to be careful around Dante when speaking of other photographers she knows. She'd have to explain she knows their work but not them personally; he has a jealous streak when he wants to have it, and she never knows when that is. Still, he insisted that she come to London on her own.

She kicks off her Nordstrom pumps. Benny Hill is on TV making faces—a half-dozen faces. He's wearing jockey shorts. Odelle takes a bath and changes into a duster. She doesn't unpack. The suitcase stands open, panty hose and panties decked across it. Something to photograph, if she had a camera.

She thinks of first coming into the lobby and spotting a man who looked just like a Russian czar, or how she imagines a Russian czar might look. But he spoke German to a little girl—a gypsy-looking little girl with black curls—who kept raising her eyebrows and shrugging her narrow shoulders.

Was haben Sie auf dem Herzen? she thought she heard.

What's on your mind?

The little girl just shrugged her shoulders again. Then a woman joined them. The woman looked Greek. A lovely woman, tall, full-figured, and fine-featured. The czar asked her something and she nodded. She seemed very aloof, then she reached out and touched the little girl's hair. Her fingers were not long and carefully manicured like you'd expect the fingers of such a woman (who looked world-traveled); they were bitten down to the quick. As she was being shown to her room, she overheard the czar asking directions of the clerk. "Which way to Knightsbridge? . . . How far? . . . And then? . . . And then . . . ?"

From the window, she looks away from the garden toward a shopping district. She can see the Russian czar, the Greek woman, and the little gypsy girl. They're waiting for a light to change, then they cross the windy street. The Greek woman wraps her long skirt around her knees to keep it from ballooning. The little girl lets hers balloon, showing starch-white panties. She can see into two of the shop windows: One has clothes that look psychedelic or like Tiffany glass. The other is some sort of gourmet grocery store with plums, cheese, and assorted breads in the window.

Hungry, she calls room service and orders onion rolls, butter, plums. She eats the plums but not the onion rolls.

She wishes she'd done more with underwater photography, but after she'd been diving with Dante and his oceanographer friends it hadn't interested her anymore. Dante had asked her to go diving again, but she wouldn't.

Dante said it had been a waste to teach her. When she came back to the States, she experimented some with microphotography. Some. And she'd gone up with a friend in an airplane and tried aerial photography. But somehow that hadn't kept her interest either. Then she had started photographing bits of seafood on a plate, half-eaten pizzas, umbrellas, cheeses, raisins, string, a screw . . .

The next morning, on a bench in Kensington Park, Odelle feeds the pigeons crumbled bits of onion rolls. Still, she hadn't called Remunda.

Such photography, though, doesn't it become mechanical? she remembered an interviewer had asked her at one of her museum showings. But dreams are so démodé, n'est-ce pas? the interviewer asked, after hearing her opinion about another photographer who made her photographs look like waking dreams. Tossing the crumbs to the pigeons, she thinks of the time she'd gone into Manhattan to an art agency with her portfolio. Her father had driven her up there from Connecticut. As they were getting out of the car, a woman brushed past them, moving quickly as if she were late for an appointment. A tall, blonde, chiseled woman. But the woman had to wait at the elevator anyway, and she and her father rode up in the elevator with her, wondering if she were a model or an actress.

She and her father took some time finding the door to the agency, but when she found it she discovered that the woman was the one she'd come to see. (Her father waited out in the waiting room when the secretary sent her in.)

The woman looked at the photographs and had seemed to like them immensely. The underwater group she liked especially; the rock that turned out to be the fish Geronimo, she liked.

"Charming," she said of another one.

Then something the woman had said. Something about having spotted her outside. Something she couldn't remember exactly. But the woman had mentioned "her driver." And she'd corrected her, saying, "That's not my driver; that's my father."

The woman had got that look. She was silent for half a moment, then she started looking at more photographs, pointing to the flaws in them.

"They're rather charming," she said, "in an amateurish sort of way, I mean. You ought to go to a good photography school. They've got a good photography school at . . ."

"I've taught there," said Odelle.

"Oh, have you? Well, just about everyone teaches there nowadays, don't they?"

Then she was sorry, but she wouldn't be able to use any of the photographs. Some were very charming, but they weren't really up to par, and nothing that hadn't been photographed before, nothing really original. She couldn't really see sending them to the ______ Gallery or any other New York gallery or anywhere else, for that matter. Then she opened a portfolio that was on her desk and held up photographs that Odelle recognized instantly as Remunda's.

"These just arrived from London," the woman said. "Now these are what you call photographs."

"How'd it go?" her father asked, when she got outside. "It didn't."

She didn't tell him about the woman having mistaken him for her driver. Or the rest of it. Nor did she tell him that the woman represented Remunda.

"Well, they're not the only agency," he'd said.

He'd taken her to a Mexican restaurant to cheer her up. Her favorite food was Mexican. She ordered a bean and cheese enchilada, and he had a plate of nachos. He had a cognac and Sprite. She had just Coke.

"I don't understand, then, why she wrote that nice letter," he said. "Having you come all the way up here for nothing."

Odelle shrugged. She said she didn't want to talk about it. The letter had indeed sounded enthusiastic, but the agent had stopped just short of committing herself to anything. She hadn't committed herself. But Odelle didn't want to think about it. But she could tell Remunda was on the tip of her father's tongue, that maybe Remunda would recommend someone, or maybe she should send some of her photographs to Remunda. Remunda had after all sent her that book of her own photographs. But he must've seen Odelle's look too, for he didn't say anything about Remunda.

Odelle had been staying with her father and Chagga at their house in New London, Connecticut. Her father had his own printing and photocopy shop, and she worked for him part time while she tried to sell her photographs. She'd sold quite a few as a freelance photographer, but her father had thought that by having the agent she'd be able to work at it full time.

"Did you tell her about the photographers' conference?" her father asked, as they were driving back.

"That doesn't mean anything," she answered. "If she didn't like the pictures."

Her father hadn't said anything else. To change the subject, she finally told him about meeting Dante. But she didn't tell him that Dante was planning to move to Manhattan and that he'd asked her to move in with him. As they slowed up for the toll bridge, she took from a pocketbook a photograph of Dante and showed him. Dante was standing on the boat with his Scandinavian friends. Her father didn't say anything except, "Oh, yeah?" Then he said, "I thought you meant some Italian."

"Naw. They're Jamaican originally. I mean. Dante's family."

He paid the toll and they entered Connecticut, driving toward New Haven.

"And that's Jomfrey from Laaland," she laughed, pointing. "And that's Gerd."

She didn't remember the names of the others. She shoved the photograph back into her purse. She could still taste the garlic from the enchilada.

"Are you in love?" he asked. She nodded.

"What?" He was looking straight ahead. "Yes," she mumbled.

"Is it the real thing?" he asked. She didn't answer.

She stands outside a tourist-shop window that displays photographs of volcanoes, pyramids, and the Aegean sea. Next door to it is a photographic gallery. In the window there are several photographs by Remunda Eadweard. So she enters.

The shop is in disarray: a few photographs have been mounted and are on the wall; others in the process of being mounted are scattered on a long wooden table; an antique couch in a corner is covered with a clear-plastic drop sheet to prevent paint stains; several parts of the floor are covered with opaque-green drop sheets. She skirts some of them to look at photographs on the far wall.

"Do you see anything you like?" the gallery director asks.

She's a woman in her mid-forties, Odelle supposes. Her hair is sun bleached and her face copper colored, as if she's just come back from a Mediterranean vacation. Though she's smiling, there're the furrows of a frown on her forehead. She's wearing a green linen skirt and a green-and-white-striped silk blouse. On her feet, she wears sneakers. She has small green eyes and severely arched eyebrows. Her small eyes give a piercing look.

"Oh, I'm just looking," says Odelle.

"American?"

"Yes. No. Yes."

The woman apologizes for everything being so untidy and explains that they're in the process of remodeling the shop. Odelle says, "That's okay," as she moves through bits of sawdust and around a wooden sawhorse to another side of the gallery. The woman follows, chatting.

"What's that word you Americans use for 'untidy?'" she asks. "It's a marvelous word."

Odelle can think of nothing but "untidy."

"No, it's a slang expression," the woman says. "You Americans use it all the time. You hardly ever say 'untidy' like we do. You use this marvelous other expression."

Odelle can only remember using the word "untidy." She says so, as she moves along photographs of milky beaches, rock formations, dreamscapes, wildernesses, and human faces.

"It's a marvelous expression," the woman repeats.

They stand silent in front of a Peruvian volcano. The photograph seems not much different from the one in the tourist window next door.

The tourist-window photographer had seemed just as conscious of being an "artist" as this one, or maybe this one had been just as conscious of being a "tour guide" as the other one. It's a nice photograph though. And there's a nice assortment of photographs. There're photographs by Italians, Japanese, a Greek, someone from Bali.

"Lived-in," the woman exclaims.

"What?"

"Lived-in. You say a thing looks 'lived-in.' We're always having Americans to the house, and they're forever using that marvelous expression . . . They like our house because it looks 'lived-in.' I know they mean untidy . . . I suppose you only say that of houses, though, don't you?"

"Houses, yes," says Odelle, as she stands before a row of photographs of famous people, then of migratory birds.

"He's a very clean photographer, don't you think?" the woman asks. "These ones here have more visual ambiguity."

She starts to lead Odelle to them, but someone else enters. "Forgive us for being so untidy," she begins, "but we're . . . renovating . . ."

Odelle looks around for the more ambiguous photographs—could they be Remunda's? Not finding them, she heads for the door.

"Come again," the woman calls.

Outside, across the street, she spots a camera shop. As she waits for the light to change, she holds onto her skirt to keep it from ballooning in the wind. She crosses the street. She doesn't like feeling camera-less. Inside the shop, she spots one of those new Japanese-made film-less cameras.

"A gift?" asks the salesman.

"Yes," she replies and allows him to wrap it.

At a newsstand, as she heads back toward the hotel, she stops and buys a copy of *Modern Photography*. There's an interview with Remunda Eadweard. She doesn't notice it until she reaches the hotel lobby, sets her package down on a writing table, and opens to the table of contents. Then she opens to the interview. Accompanying the interview is a photograph, but it's not a recent photograph; it's Remunda in the 1960s. Remunda is sitting at a table, but you can't see the table.

In the left-hand bottom corner, you can see the tops of what look like China teacups. Remunda has her hands forward, thumbs pointed up, gesticulating as she speaks. In reality, they're smallish hands, but the photograph makes them look large.

Perhaps she's at some conference or speaking to a photography class.

No, no photography class, thinks Odelle. Probably some political rally. Her sleek black hair is parted in the middle and reaches beyond her shoulders. She has high fine cheekbones; large black eyes and thick, black eyelashes; a full mouth, the top lip larger than the bottom; a longish but nicely shaped nose; and large ears. She isn't looking at the camera but away, toward the group she's speaking to. There's the hint of a smile.

The interviewer, in prefacing notes, calls her a photographer *engagée*, using the French word for "committed." She's never really thought of herself, though, as "political" or "radical," Remunda says, but she's concerned about "injustices" and often finds herself in places where some sort of "social revolution" is going on; her photographic style, she admits, is rather eclectic, but she can see a thematic thread. Then there's a quote from her, about believing that some ethical system is necessary "in order to take soundings. Aesthetics without ethics is a sign of immaturity." Odelle looks for the quotation in the interview but can't find it. In the interview, the interviewer mentions a recent divorce to which Remunda doesn't reply; instead, she directs the woman back to discussing the photography, the "work"—not her personal life, not her biography.

Odelle half expects to find her own name in the interview or the name of her father, but she knows she won't. She thinks of the photography book Remunda has sent her, but no letters, no postcards. She thinks of the New York agent and wonders what the agent would have said if she'd said, "The man you thought was my driver used to be her husband." Probably she'd have done nothing. Probably she simply wouldn't have believed her.

"You were in Cuba during the revolution," the interviewer comments. "Well, it wasn't during the revolution actually. It was shortly afterwards."

The interviewer says that the photographs taken in Cuba look as if they were taken right in the midst of it.

"And you went to Mexico after you heard about the massacre of Tlatelolco."

"Yes," is Remunda's only answer.

"Do you believe there's such a thing as a political aesthetic?" the woman asks.

Remunda says she doesn't know.

"But that's your term," the interviewer says.

Remunda says she doesn't remember saying that. All in all, it's not one of Remunda's best interviews. Odelle has read other interviews where Remunda has spoken more freely and fully and forcefully and sounds more profound. There are rumors that Remunda was under some sort of surveillance after she'd taken a series of photographs of British troops against the bleak landscape of Northern Ireland. Odelle has never seen the photographs and feels that it's only a rumor, anyway, for Remunda still seems to travel about as freely as ever. That she's never come to the US surprises her. There are enough bleak landscapes there. Perhaps she's been there and simply never looked her up. No, she'd have looked her up. She won't believe otherwise. But she's not even sure that she'll find Remunda in London. She should have called ahead and made real plans.

She rereads parts of the interview:

INTERVIEWER: Tell me something about yourself, when you started photographing.

REMUNDA: During the war. I was seventeen. I had a camera and I photographed people in the bombing shelters. And then when we came up out of the shelters, I'd photograph the destruction, the bombed-out buildings, the faces of the people. Once a journalist from the Associated Press, I believe, spotted me taking pictures and wanted to see some of them. So some of my pictures accompanied one of his stories and so things began. I didn't want to be a photographic journalist though.

INTERVIEWER: Why not?

REMUNDA: I didn't like the captions they put under the pictures. For me, the pictures always said more. I prefer the pictures to speak for themselves. Photographs are like texts, you know. They should speak for themselves.

INTERVIEWER: Is that why you never name your photographs?

REMUNDA: Yes. I used to name them sparingly, but now I don't name them at all.

INTERVIEWER: Do you think that being a woman has restricted you as a photographer?

REMUNDA: Being a woman is work, is a lot of work. I suppose being a photographer has restricted me in being a woman rather than the other way around. Or rather I should say being a wife.

INTERVIEWER: You were recently divorced.

REMUNDA: Yes. But let's not talk about it. I'd rather talk about the work.

INTERVIEWER: You never talk about yourself.

REMUNDA: No. Or just what impinges on photography. My marriage, my divorce really doesn't have to do with the photographs.

INTERVIEWER: Do you consider yourself a feminist?

REMUNDA: I'm interested in what it means to be a woman in the modern world. Or maybe the world in general, whether modern or ancient. Or throughout history. But I don't believe that looking at my photographs one can tell whether a man or woman took them. When I simply use my initials on them, most people think a man took them. I remember once someone tried to compliment me by telling me I take photos like a man.

INTERVIEWER: Like when they tell lady writers, "You write like a man," and it's intended as a compliment.

REMUNDA: Exactly.

INTERVIEWER: Do you think men take better photographs than women?

REMUNDA: Uh, they seem to find themselves in more interesting places, don't you think?

INTERVIEWER: There seems to be a certain intimacy in your photographs that I don't believe a man could get, interesting place or not. Don't you think so?

REMUNDA: Do you think so? I believe that women should be totally free and have all the rights of a man.

INTERVIEWER: That's a feminist manifesto if I ever heard one.

REMUNDA: Feminist journals have used my photographs, and I don't object when women's groups want to use them . . . There's much sexism . . . I've been among a lot of revolutionaries, men winning their freedom, but even among revolutionaries, there's much sexism. Even when the women fight along with the men, in Cuba, in Vietnam, in China . . . There's so much sexism everywhere . . . The revolutionary leaders I've met have always been very kind to me. But even that's a form of sexism, wouldn't you say? I was with a bunch of other photographers once, male photographers, and the revolutionary leader pointed to me and said, "I want her." That's sexism too, wouldn't you say?

INTERVIEWER: But you're a great photographer. Who are some other photographers that you admire?
REMUNDA: The brave ones.

Remunda named a Chilean photographer who took great "social photographs" and who had been very vocal in her opposition to the United States. She'd "disappeared" after the Allende regime, but curiously some of her photographs had begun to reappear in spots and places, though no one could locate the Chilean photographer herself. She also admired a certain Cuban photographer, a man she'd met after the Cuban revolution. She named an Algerian photographer and a Bolivian. The interviewer asked her whether there were any European photographers that she admired, but she didn't reply. She named a Tanzanian photographer instead.

INTERVIEWER: Of all the photographs that you've taken, which ones do you most admire?
REMUNDA: The ones that haven't been published or exhibited yet.
INTERVIEWER: You mean the ones that haven't been taken yet?
REMUNDA: No. They've been taken. But the journals and the galleries won't use them.
INTERVIEWER: You photographed the Blue Men.
REMUNDA: Yes.
INTERVIEWER: Explain to our readers who they are, so they won't think you mean the Smurfs.
REMUNDA: The Smurfs?
INTERVIEWER: Never mind.
REMUNDA: Well, the Blue Men, actually the MOREHOB, were an independence movement in the Spanish Sahara in the 1960s. What used to be the Spanish Sahara. They fought against Spain, or rather Spanish rule. It's now Maurita-

nia. They didn't get their independence until 1972 though. Eduardo Moha was their leader. I photographed them, but I didn't publish or exhibit any of the photographs until after they got their independence.

INTERVIEWER: You helped a lot of the refugees.

REMUNDA: No, there were thousands of refugees. There was not a lot one person could do. I contributed some of my income to one of the refugee camps in Morocco. But there's not a lot one person can do. That's why I joined Amnesty International. I'm reading bios they've sent me . . .

INTERVIEWER: You ought to write your autobiography. It would be very interesting . . . er . . . Tell me some more of your adventures.

REMUNDA: I wouldn't exactly call them adventures.

INTERVIEWER: What would you call them?

REMUNDA: Most of the people I photograph lead rather difficult lives. I don't know what sort of person would call it an adventure to be among them. Not the sort of person I am. Or the sort of person I try to be.

INTERVIEWER: Uh, yes. One critic said your photographs always involve some sort of moral dilemma. Even those that look quite ordinary, I mean, on the surface.

REMUNDA: I don't know.

INTERVIEWER: Er. There's nothing extraneous in your photographs. That's what I like. Or rather, what seems extraneous belongs there. Uh, how did you get to be so *engagée*? From what I know of your family, they're rather conservative types from Devon.

REMUNDA: People are different. I developed a social conscience when I was quite young.

INTERVIEWER: You don't look like a radical.

REMUNDA: How's a radical supposed to look? . . . I just never wanted to be a bat.

INTERVIEWER: What?

REMUNDA: I'm thinking of a quote I read once by Samuel Coleridge, one of the things that stuck. He said, ". . . the great majority of men live like bats, but in twilight, and know and feel the philosophy of their age only by its reflections and refractions . . ." And of course, you can say the same about women. And there's another quotation that stuck too. One from Pope: "Most souls, 'tis true, but peep out once an age."

INTERVIEWER: Um, yes, quite right . . .

REMUNDA: Or perhaps it was just the war.

INTERVIEWER: A lot of people went through the war and it didn't turn them into radicals.

REMUNDA: But it changed them. I mean, the ones who were spoiled. I'm thinking of something from Hemingway now. One of his characters says, "I wanted to try this new drink. That's all we do, isn't it?—look at things and try new drinks." That's the sort of people I mean. The Great Depression changed a lot of people like that, and then the war changed others.

INTERVIEWER: Er, do you think you'll spend more time in London?

REMUNDA: Yes, I love London. You couldn't have been here during the war and not love London. I was born here, after all. But I would like to go to China, to go back to Vietnam, back to Africa, maybe Ethiopia. I'd like to go to Cuba again too . . . for the anniversary of the revolution. But I love London. They wanted to send me out of London during the war, to the country, when they were sending a lot of

> the children to the country. But I refused to go. I stayed here and took pictures. I was here during the Blitz. I took pictures. I couldn't not love London. I fell in love for the first time, too, during the war.

But she didn't tell the interviewer about it. She said nothing further.

Odelle reads the interview over again, trying to find herself or her father between the lines.

Remunda and her father had met during the war in one of the bombing shelters, during an air raid. He was eighteen, but he looked younger. He'd looked about sixteen. He'd looked too young to be a soldier. She'd photographed him. They'd started talking. She kept taking photographs of others, but she kept finding her way back to him. They talked about the war and movies and her photographs and where each was from. She said she'd heard of Kentucky, because of the Derby or the "Darby" as she pronounced it. They were both so young. But the war made them seem older. Her favorite movie stars were Americans: William Powell, Jean Arthur, Myrna Loy, John Garfield. She said he looked a bit like John Garfield, except for being "colored," which was the word she used then. No one down in the shelter seemed to bother that they formed a couple; it was only when they came up out of the shelter that there were the wrong looks and the people trying to bust them up. After the baby was born, he wanted to return to the States, but she wanted to stay in London. And besides London, there were other places she wanted to go, places you couldn't take a baby anyway. Odelle didn't know all the story. Her father wouldn't tell her all of it. She just knew that her father had taken her back to the States, to Covington, Kentucky, with him. When she was about ten or twelve, he'd taken her on a vacation to Martinique, where he met Chagga.

When they returned to the States, Chagga came with them. They stayed for a while in Covington, but then her father decided to move north to Connecticut, to a town called New London. He opened a print shop in the basement of their house. Chagga worked part time in a dance studio teaching African dance and studied business at a local college.

But after the war, for a few months, he'd had an idyllic time with Remunda. They went to movies and restaurants, for walks in gardens, rides along the moors that he'd only read about in books. And they worked together too, clearing away rubble in the after-the-war effort to rebuild London. He had proposed to her in the bombing shelter, but it was only after the war, in the Kensington Gardens, that she'd answered yes.

When Odelle was a little girl, she used to ask question after question about Remunda.

"She said I looked like John Garfield."

"Who's that?"

"A famous movie actor. Way before your time."

"I remember."

"You can't remember before your time."

"On TV you can."

They'd laughed and he lifted her onto his shoulders. But her father didn't look a bit like John Garfield. Not a bit. Maybe Remunda just wanted him to look like John Garfield, on account of the war and all. But he couldn't explain it to her, not back then, how couples would form during a war—people who maybe wouldn't have gotten together before or after it.

Years later, in college, when she'd read Woolf or Bowen, she'd try to imagine what Remunda was like. But there weren't any radicals in Woolf or Bowen. At least none that she recognized as radicals.

Returned to her hotel room, Odelle throws *Modern Photography* into her suitcase and tears the new camera from its gift wrappings. She thinks of how, when she was little, she used to sit out in the sun all day, trying to get dark, so she'd look more like her father's complexion. But it didn't work. And she used to have temper tantrums, her father said. But she refused to remember them.

Finally, she picks up the phone. "Remunda . . . Remunda Eadweard."

"Yes?"

"This is Odelle . . ."

There is no hesitation in her welcome. "Odelle! Where are you? Are you in London?"

"London. Yes."

"Why didn't you . . . ? Why don't you . . . ?" She's silent for a moment. "What hotel?"

"The Royal Garden."

Remunda says nothing for a moment. Perhaps, Odelle is thinking, she should have stayed at a less luxurious hotel, a more proletarian hotel. She thinks fleetingly of something Sartre had said, some question he had posed. In one of her classes at college they'd read his essay "Black Orpheus" and argued over the question: "What will happen if, casting off his negritude for the sake of the revolution, the black man no longer wishes to consider himself only a part of the proletariat?" Perhaps Remunda is thinking the hotel isn't "revolutionary" enough.

"How nice," she says finally.

"Where should we meet?" Odelle asks.

"Why don't I come there?" asks Remunda. "Things are a bit untidy here, at the moment. I've just divorced, again, and . . . well . . . I've just come back from Devon too. That's where your grandmother lives . . ."

Odelle is silent. She's never even thought of relatives on Remunda's side. Well, she's thought of them abstractly, not as concrete, palpable human beings.

"Untidy doesn't bother me," she says. "But we could meet at a restaurant or something. Do you know the Caprice?"

"What?"

"This book that suggests restaurants . . . I was skimming this book . . . I mean, for tourists."

"On Arlington Street. Yes," says Remunda. "Or we could go to Bill Bentley's. They've got excellent fish. Or, there's a Thai restaurant, if you'd like. Excellent food. I go there a lot. It reminds me of Bangkok. But the Caprice is good. We'll meet at the Caprice. Do you know how to get to Arlington Street? I don't think it's far from the Royal Garden."

"Oh, yes, I can find my way," says Odelle.

"Good."

Then Remunda mentions the Gandhi, an Indian restaurant on Villiers Street. Then she says again, "But the Caprice is fine . . . Do you like king prawns?"

"What?"

"King prawns?"

"Sure."

"Should I come for you?"

Odelle repeats that she can find her way.

"Oh, sure, of course you can, Odelle."

Odelle thinks of sitting with her father in a burger place in Connecticut. At the table behind them a man was talking to a woman. The woman didn't say a word, or the woman had murmured so lowly that they'd just heard the man.

"Oh, come off it."

. . . .

"Oh, get with it."

. . . .

"Oh, get with it."

. . . .

"Oh, come off it."

"The Caprice is fine," Remunda says.

Her father had told her of falling in love with Remunda along with her "bedtime stories," and he used to occasionally show her some of the photographs Remunda had taken. She remembered one of them, a series of them taken in Brazil among the poor of Brazil. Those Remunda had named "The River of January," which was, of course, the English translation of Rio de Janeiro. They were photographs of little boys and girls about her age, street urchins.

"Why didn't she stay with you?" Odelle had asked.

Her father had merely shown her the photographs—as if they were an answer.

"Didn't she love you enough?" Odelle had asked. But her father hadn't answered.

When he married Chagga, though, he stopped telling her about Remunda, and sometimes Chagga would take over the bedtime stories and tell her African folktales of elephants, lions, monkeys, and such. Or she would tell her heroic stories of Mwindo and Ozidi and Sunjata. But Chagga was also a great fan of the blues and used to like to listen to all the great blues singers and sometimes she would go around humming a song by Sippie Wallace called "Women Be Wise, Don't Advertise Your Man." And she liked rock too, all kinds, from Tina Turner's "Paradise Is Here" to Chris Rea's "Windy Town." James Brown was her all-time favorite singer, though. And she liked the new music, the rap.

She also told Odelle about the Whydah slave traders and about the Fon army and of how in the seventeenth and eighteenth centuries King Agaja helped to put an end to the slave trade and of how there were not only white slave traders but Black ones too. (Chagga's middle name was Ouidah, which she said was the same as Whydah; she had ancestors from both Mali and Dahomey.) So King Agaja not only had to fight against the white slave traders but against the Black slave traders too. She told of how there were also women in the Fon army and that one of her great ancestors was one of those warrior women. Odelle had only thought of Amazon-type women as fighting in armies and wondered whether Chagga's great ancestress was as small as she was. Though her family had moved to Martinique when she was quite small, she had returned to Africa to attend African colleges. She had gone to the Haile Selassie I University at Addis Ababa; she had been to the University of Dar es Salaam in Tanzania; she had gone to Fourah Bay College in Freetown, Sierra Leone, and the University of Nairobi in Kenya. She talked of joining a group of fisherwomen and fishing along the coasts of Zanzibar. She talked of working on a clove plantation. She had stayed longest in Zanzibar and had almost married a Kikuyu. She spoke of the Maji Maji war against the German colonialists in 1906. (Her lover's father had fought in it.) She talked of riding a crowded train from Arusha, Tanzania, to Southern Kenya. She talked of returning to Mali to visit relatives, who were Mandinka. Some of her relatives, she said, claimed to be descendants of the great fourteenth-century ruler Mansa Musa. She spoke of working in a textile factory while in Mali and in another factory that processed rice. Though her own family could be called well-to-do by Martinican standards, she had wanted to learn to see things from the bottom up, so to speak. She spoke of Jenne and Gao and Timbuktu, not only the modern cities but the ancient ones.

She had told neither Chagga nor her father about the trip to London.

On the airplane, she'd listened to the conversations of two women in the row behind her:

"Who was it said hell was a city much like London? Byron, wasn't it?"

"Or Shelley. But it could've been Byron. It sounds like Byron."

"No, it sounds like Shelley too."

One of the women had never before been to London. But the other one had been there just before the war, she said. She was a young woman; her father worked for an international commercial house. They left, though, before things got too dreadful. Before the war they used to travel a lot. They'd been to Berlin, to Amsterdam, to Madrid, to Rome.

Because her father worked for this international company, people thought they were rich. But they weren't rich. And she still wasn't rich. People thought because she still went abroad that she was rich. But no, she wasn't. She was just a woman with simple tastes. Where others bought extravagant things, she spent her money on travel.

But you've got sumptuous things, you've got extravagant things, the other woman countered.

Oh, those are gifts. Those are all gifts from people I knew before the war. We weren't rich. But people liked to give us things. I don't know why.

And then from things, they started talking about a man. She couldn't tell whether it was the husband of the one or the other.

Sergio doesn't express love easily. When he loves a person, he sort of loves them from the inside.

She'd wanted to listen to more, more about Sergio and Berlin and London and Rome and Madrid, but the plane was landing and the women were gathering their things.

And Chagga liked "Wodka Wyborowa"—the "best Polish vodka." It had surprised her the first time she heard Chagga ask for it. They had gone out to a restaurant together for lunch, when she was older. Chagga had come to visit her at school and they'd gone together to this little restaurant, a place where the people seemed not used to Black people. Alone, she didn't have the same problem, but with Chagga there the waiter seemed to be behaving in a kind of vexed, impatient way.

"Are you done?" he'd asked.

Chagga always left bits of food on her plate.

"No, please bring me some Wodka Wyborowa. A bottle," she said.

"We don't serve liquor in here."

"But those ladies have Scotch . . ." She pointed up ahead.

"They always bring their own bottle—the boss lets 'em. They're harmless."

"Another cup of tea, then."

When the waiter left, Chagga mumbled, "No one's harmless."

The owner of the restaurant was Polish and German, but most of the artifacts in the restaurant were German—German landscapes and prickets, those fifteenth-century German candlesticks.

From where she was sitting she could see a man and woman. The man's hand under the table found the woman's knee. She kept an indifferent look, but her nose quivered. The woman kept looking straight ahead, but the man kept looking in all directions till he spotted her. He gave one of those barely perceptible jumps, but he kept his hand on the woman's knee. Finally, the woman laughed, showing yellowish teeth.

That night she dreams not of Remunda, but Dante. They're at an underwater concert. The instrumentalists are wearing scuba gear and playing harps. Jazz, not classical. In the dream, though, she has not yet met Dante. She's one of the spectators. The spectators do not sit under water but watch the musicians from behind glass.

When the concert is over, a man behind her whispers something.

She turns and it's Dante.

"I didn't hear you," she says.

"I said I love you," he says.

Then they're walking along a beach, a stretch of sand on Paradise Island. He has her by the arm and is pulling her along.

"Why are you pulling me?" she asks. He keeps pulling her along with him. "Why are you pulling me?" she asks.

"Because I don't want you to run out on me," he says.

"Then I should be pulling you," she answers.

In the dream, he says his name is Dante Asante, but in truth it's Dante St. Maarten.

In the next scene they're at the Junkanoo Festival, wearing masks. They're not observers but participants. From the Junkanoo Festival, she moves through a whirlwind of scenes: in one they're playing racquetball, in another they're at Cable Beach in a casino.

"But you don't look like a gambler," Dante says.

Then they're walking along Bay Street and Dante is carrying his bag of sponges.

"Don't you want to know who I am?" he asks.

Then she's sitting at the kitchen table in the Connecticut house, she and Chagga.

"You were a fubsy baby," Chagga keeps saying.

"You didn't know me when I was a baby," she keeps replying. There are china cups on the table, and Chagga keeps talking, gesticulating with her hands.

"This is poteen," she says, pointing to the china cups. "I've made it too sweet, haven't I?"

"It is sweet," answered Odelle. "But it's good."

Chagga looks a good ten years younger than her actual age, but in the dream, as in reality, she's talking about retiring.

"Maybe I'll work a little with your father in his printing business, so I won't get bored. Or I could fish all day. Are you going to marry this Don The?"

"Dante."

"And he's fond of music, did you say?"

"He composes it."

"Well, a man whose first love is music can't be all bad."

Odelle wakes up. After dressing, she goes to the dining room for toast and coffee. Only the czar, the little gypsy, and the woman are there. They seem to be having a spirited conversation in German, but she can't make out much of it. She hears only:

"Sie ist in anderen Umständen. Ruhe!"

"Er ist hier unbekannt. Ruhe!"

She tries to remember her schoolgirl German: "*Ruhe*" meant "quiet"! He is unknown here. Who was unknown there? Something about other circumstances.

It had been Chagga more than her father who had objected to her moving to New York without being married to Dante. Chagga Jaguarundi, a small, dark woman with peppercorn hair. Her ancestors were from Mali, Mali and Dahomey. It was Chagga who taught her how to play Chinese checkers though. They were playing Chinese checkers when she told Chagga she planned to move to Manhattan with Dante. Chagga threw up her hands.

"Ils s'étaient rencontrés et tout de suite, ils s'aimèrent," exclaimed Chagga.

"But you met my father and all of a sudden fell in love," Odelle said. She remembered how there'd never been any feeling of jealousy, typical in such situations, that she'd liked Chagga right off.

"My ears are very small, but there's room for anything you've got to tell me," Chagga had said once.

And Chagga fixed them goulash and mandarin oranges and cookies shaped like shields. And it was Chagga who took her to the Ballet de l'Opera de Shanghai, which had come to town to perform.

"Ah, to dance like that," Chagga had said. As her father on the other side of her looked enraptured, not at the ballet company, but at Chagga.

And that was the first time that Odelle had really listened to music—or tried to. The music had seemed all rolled up, and when the dancing started, it opened. In masks, the dancers danced. One woman threw a tantrum, pulled her mask from her face, and rushed offstage. It didn't seem like a scene she'd seen for the first time, but one she'd always been watching, but couldn't place where.

The first dream she'd had after she'd met Dante was about masks.

She was at a costume party and a masked man came to talk to her. "I thought I'd meet you again," he said. "I always thought so."

Odelle, masked herself, insisted that she was the wrong masked woman. But she refused to take her mask off to prove she was not the one he remembered.

"Where did you go?" he asked.

In the dream, she wanted to wonder something, but couldn't think what to wonder. What should a woman wonder about a masked man? she asked herself. So she decided to wonder whether or not he was dangerous. He started to tell her the story of them, of their love affair, but she refused to listen. She stared into the bottom of her rum glass.

"Do you want to dance?" he asked.

"What do you mean, dance?" she asked.

"You're as cruel as ever," he said.

"Man, I don't know you," she said.

Chagga, wearing a mask—she can always tell Chagga, masked or not—comes over to rescue her. Eager to introduce her to an Englishwoman she pulls her away from the masked man.

"I'd like you to meet . . ."

"*Enchanté*," said Odelle before she could hear the woman's name. The mask the woman is wearing is made out of straw.

"She's a gold miner," explains Chagga. "Just returned from the Amazon."

"Did you discover any gold?" Odelle asked.

"Actually, no gold, but plenty of . . ."

"Straw?" Odelle asked.

"No, fevers I was going to say, actually. We were reduced to eating lizards and wild onions and green lemons. But I won't bore you with that story."

Then suddenly it was Odelle wearing the straw mask. The other masked guests encircled her like she was an object of curiosity or mystery or speculation. Then they began to decorate her with shells and birds' feathers. They lined up to adorn her with these things. She felt terrified, more terrified than anything, but she didn't know the source of her terror.

"Have no fear," Chagga whispered beside her.

The people in line were no longer holding shells and birds' feathers but bows, arrows, shields, spears, swords, clubs.

"Are you sure?" Odelle asked.

"Yes," replied Chagga. "You have only to put on your mask."

"But I already have it on," said Odelle.

"I mean your own," said Chagga. "I mean your own."

Then she was in her own mask again, but it was a new mask, one made of a feather, a jewel, a shell, a shield, and even a spear.

The original masked man was standing in front of her now, holding a spear, and she realized it was Dante. He leaned forward and kissed her, but it was no ordinary kiss; it was a ritual of kissing. When he finished kissing her, he asked, "May I lift this mask?"

"Yes," she answered.

He tried to lift it, but it stuck. "It hurts," she said.

They discovered at the same time that she wasn't wearing a mask at all, but her real face.

She woke up.

At the photographers' conference in the Bahamas, she'd seen a woman from a distance. Dark-haired. She thought for a moment it might be her; it might be Remunda. But the woman was younger, much younger than Remunda could have been.

When Odelle was sitting in a restaurant on Paradise Island, she spotted the woman again. The woman was drinking too much and looking peevish. She was eating grouper with onions, green pepper, and garlic.

She finished one drink and then ordered another. She didn't eat the grouper but played with it with her fork. When she spotted Odelle watching her so absurdly, she wiggled her little finger.

She wiggled her little finger for Odelle to come over and join her. But she reminded her too much of Remunda, how Remunda must have looked at that age. Odelle started toward her, almost got to the table, and then rushed past.

But the woman didn't let her go. She rushed outside and grabbed hold of her arm and they walked together along the beach. The woman was tipsy and kept holding onto her arm. The woman wore high-heeled pumps; she kicked them off and walked barefoot.

Odelle told the woman about meeting Dante. She talked to her as if she'd known her always. And the woman told her about one of her early lovers, someone not at all like Dante, a violent man who when he got into rages would break her cameras. She'd come to Nassau not really for the photographers' conference but to regroup, to re-assemble herself.

She kept waiting for the woman to ask why she'd run when she saw her, to ask who she reminded her of, but she never did. She kept waiting for the woman to ask her who she was, but she never did. She talked about her own bad love affair, how she hadn't wanted to take the chance with anyone else, for fear they'd be like that. Destroyers, she called them. Maybe they all might not destroy your cameras, but cameras were just a metaphor. Men were just destroyers, she'd thought, but then she was sitting on the beach here, just this morning, and she saw this lovely Bahamian couple and the man stood up and took the woman's hand and they ran into the sea together. The woman didn't know how to swim and so she was holding onto his shoulders, and they swam together like that, the woman riding on top of him. It was lovely to watch. Well, at first she thought the woman didn't know how to swim, but then the woman let go and swam on her own. Then they were swimming side by side. It was lovely to watch. And then she felt, after watching a couple like that, that there were men out there, not all destroyers, men one could enjoy. But instead of going out and enjoying them, she'd gone and got drunk. But it was good to watch, she said, good to watch.

Her look was smug, then cynical, then just high. But it was good to watch, she repeated.

And she talked about all sorts of things: Her name was Clio and she was from New Orleans and her father was a maker of Mardi Gras costumes; their family on her father's side had been makers of Mardi Gras costumes for generations. She liked kiwi fruit with her ice cream. Her favorite director was a Swedish woman named Zetterling. Had Odelle seen her new film? Then she talked about the man again and how Sartre said that hell was other people.

But we're our own hells, too, Odelle put in.

Clio said nothing. She just gave that look, smug and cynical and high.

Odelle kept looking about the hotel room for samples of Clio's photographs but didn't see any. She just saw the hotel's photograph of a colorful sailboat riding the waves, a sailboat that looked so light, so airy.

She started to tell Clio about herself but instead mumbled something about modern naval design.

But Clio had really tied one on, and when she fell asleep, Odelle tiptoed out of the hotel room. The next day, when she saw her in one of the conference rooms, the woman pretended not to know Odelle.

"Clio . . ."

"What? My name's not Clio; it's Clare. Clare Ronin."

She stayed to see Clare show some of her photographs and give her talk. The series of photographs was called "The Origins of Sins," and they showed innocent-faced children. "Most people forget childhood," Clare was saying, "and remember childhood as innocent. Or perhaps it's simply because they think compared with adult sins, the sins of childhood seem like innocence. But it's the origins of all sins: pride, jealousy, lust . . . All of them, except maybe adultery."

Someone gave a low laugh.

Clare said, "When you were a child, adults always said, 'Remember your table manners.' When you grow up, you discover it's all table manners."

Odelle didn't stay to hear anymore.

You resemble him a lot," says Remunda. "But as much me. Well, if I were younger it would be about like looking into a mirror."

Then she starts talking about a new country she was going to, where they'd overthrown the government.

"People couldn't even have ordinary conversations without looking over their shoulders. Governments have to be respecters of people . . . For them, though, it's not a question of governing a country; it's a question of creating a country first . . . But this sort of stuff doesn't interest you, does it?"

Odelle says nothing, then she says, "Yes, oh yes, it does."

But she wants most of all to hear Remunda say something about her father. Not just that she resembles him but something other. But Remunda doesn't. And the only thing she says about the war is a casual remark when she orders a dessert of sliced bananas. She talks about how much she loves bananas, of how abundant potatoes were during the war and how scarce bananas. And of eating bread without butter.

"That makes bananas seem like such a luxury."

Odelle starts to tell Remunda about Chagga, her father's new wife, but instead tells her about Dante.

"Have you had pepper pot stew?" Remunda asks. She picks at the collar of a cotton blouse that looks brand-new. She wears a wool sweater. "That's a delicious Bahamian dish.

I was there years ago. Back in the fifties. I remember it like it was yesterday, though. East Beach, Crab Cay, Portuguese glass fishing boats. I can still taste the green turtle pie and hot bird peppers. Black people weren't allowed to stay in the hotels, you know; they stayed in boarding houses. So I rebelled. I refused to stay in the hotels too; I stayed in one of the boarding houses with the Blacks, with this marvelous woman who made green turtle pie. Do you know Riding Rock Wall? No? I remember riding on this flat-top boat toward Riding Rock Wall. I did a little underwater photography. You have to photograph in flat water; otherwise the pictures don't come out right. So we were in this flat-top boat heading toward flat water. No, it wasn't a pontoon boat. They called it something else, I think. Well maybe it was a pontoon boat. It was a thirty-four-foot boat; I remember that. They didn't have computer-processed images in those days, no. So you had to be in flat water. I've a photograph of a little girl at the Straw Market. Making straw dolls. She reminded me of you. I mean how I thought you'd look. I thought you would darken as you got older. We both did."

Then she looks as if that wasn't at all the thing to say. (Or Odelle imagines it.) Then she shows her photographs of a man who'd just been freed from a prison in El Salvador.

". . . hot and cold extremes, electric shocks, hot chili powder and carbonated mineral water squirted up his nose. He had to stand for hours and hours . . . But this doesn't interest you . . ."

"Yes, it does," says Odelle.

"Yes, of course," says Remunda. "How could you be human and it not?"

Then she talks about Mexico, Guatemala, the Philippines, Nicaragua, Korea (North and South), South Africa, Liberia, Albania, Argentina, Bolivia, Chile, Ethiopia, Haiti, Italy, the Netherlands, Australia, Belgium. And she has that half-smile that Odelle remembers from the photograph.

Odelle stares at the tops of the china teacups. She waits to be told about the bombing shelter, about London during the war (something more than potatoes and bananas and bread and butter). She waits to be told about being in love. And then she thinks about another dream she had, the sort that Dante would call a lucid dream, the sort you're supposed to learn from.

She was in a bombing shelter and there was a man standing there, against the wall, and he had a hat pulled down over his eyes. She knew it was Dante, but the man refused to raise his hat so that she could make out his features.

"If I raise my hat," he said, "I fear you'll wake up again."

"What do you want?" she asked.

He refused to answer. Instead, he gave her a game that one plays with a ball and stars. She didn't know the name of the game, except she once saw it in a comic book. So, she kept waiting for the comic book, but he wouldn't hand it over. She was sure it was rolled up and stuck in his inside jacket pocket. She thought that if she reached for it her own self, she'd wake up, so she continued to content herself with the ball and stars.

"When are you going to fall in love with me?" she asked.

"I've been wanting to," he said, "but I fear I'll wake."

"But shouldn't we dare it?" she asked. "Shouldn't we dare it even if it does mean waking?"

And when you mastered the lucid dream, Dante had said, you could guide it wherever you wanted it to go.

Just when she thought she had mastered the dream, she wasn't in the shelter with Dante but with her father. They were on the Ohio River in a houseboat. (For a while, he and Chagga and Odelle had lived in a houseboat.) He was whittling her a wooden horse from scraps of wood from the mill where he worked part time.

"Do you want a rocking horse or a regular horse?" he asked.

"A regular horse," she replied.

When he finished, they brushed enamel on it together. He used the large brush and she the tiny one. She worried him to let her use the large brush. He relented, but she discovered that it was too heavy for her tiny hand. It took a whole minute before she, shamefaced, told him what the problem was, and they exchanged brushes.

The horse stood drying while her father made its saddle from leather odds and ends. She stood by, impatient to ride. When her father finished making the saddle and bridle and the horse was dried, he strapped the saddle on the wooden horse, fixed the bridle, and lifted her into the saddle. She grabbed hold of the bridle and shouted, "Get up." She shouted, "Get up," again. She snapped the bridle and shouted again, "Get up." She shouted, "Get up."

They both knew then that it was really the rocking horse she'd meant to ask for, but when her father offered to modify it, she stubbornly refused.

And in the next stage of the dream, Chagga was in the kitchen of Dante's Bahamas house. She was peeling a banana and bending forward and feeding a monkey, which reached its tiny hands up. It was a spider monkey. Then the kitchen dissolved and became a tree-lined square in the center of an artificial park. Beyond the park were round, thatch-roofed houses and a few long ones with geometric, painted designs that looked Moorish. Other monkeys paraded about the square, being fed by other visitors or simply promenading or climbing trees.

"These are sacred monkeys," Chagga said. "I wonder if they know they're sacred . . . They probably do."

She took out a new banana and peeled it. While the monkey waited to be fed, she ate it herself. The monkey watched her suspiciously, then paraded off to be fed by a visiting other.

As they left the square, Chagga said to a group of monkeys, who stood together chattering, "Amusez-vous bien."

Then she told Odelle about other villages with other sacred animals, which the villagers treated like human beings.

She asked Odelle if she had ever heard of the word "totem." And suddenly Odelle can't remember if it was a dream or something that really happened. But the other part, Odelle was certain, was a dream. She looked up and saw a striking, high-cheekboned woman, hair shaved above her ears but the top bushy, ears dangling with conch-shell earrings.

The woman was entering the park. She thought the woman was African and told Chagga how striking she was. Chagga informed her that the woman was one of the girls who came with the Peace Corps and stayed. She kept looking at the woman and realized that the woman was Remunda, except with dark skin. She looked away for a moment, and when she glanced back, the woman had disappeared, but the group of chattering monkeys had grown by one. She was about to tell Chagga how something supernatural had happened, but then she spotted the woman again at the end of the park, feeding one of the sacred monkeys. She still marvels at how it could have been Remunda, if only Remunda were darker.

"They've grown very cunning and clever," Chagga said, speaking of the sacred monkeys.

Then Odelle woke up inside the dream but realized that she was still sleeping. There was a labyrinth of spiraling staircases. She kept moving.

No, it was more like a maze of spiraling staircases, spirals and circles, moving in every direction. You think you're climbing in one direction and you're spiraled in another. She saw Dante at the top of some stairs. He told her to come up. She tried to explain to him that these weren't ordinary stairs, that she couldn't simply move toward him and be assured that she'd get there.

"You'll have to fly," he said.

"How can I fly?" she asked.

"You've got wings," he said.

She realized that she did have them, but she didn't know what to do with them.

"It's easy," he said. "Just jump up."

She jumped up and moved toward him. Then she woke up.

I've not seen a camera like that," says Remunda, noticing Odelle's.

She lifts it toward her and peers into the lens.

"It's just on the market," says Odelle. "It's new. It's filmless."

"Filmless? Just what I need. X-rays ruin film, you know."

"X-rays?"

"Airport X-rays, you know. I always take my film out of the bag every time I travel, right at the checkpoint, and have 'em checked separately, but most places they give you such a hassle, I just let it go through."

"What do X-rays do to film?" Odelle asks.

"Spoil the tint, dear. Spoil the tint." She half-smiles. "All the photos I took in Soweto were ruined. They gave me such a hassle, such a hassle you wouldn't believe."

Then she starts talking about photographing a certain Indian tribe in Guatemala. They stained themselves with the juice of the genipapo.

Genipapo is a green juice that dries black. For nine days, it will not wash off. They slept in hammocks. To get in their good graces, she'd stained herself with genipapo. For nine whole days, it wouldn't wash off. So she just stayed in the jungle. She wouldn't dare go back to Guatemala City looking like that.

"Did you get a picture of yourself looking like that?" asks Odelle.

"I certainly wish I had," Remunda laughs. "But you wouldn't have known me. You wouldn't have known me at all."

It is when the laugh turns into a half-smile that Odelle snaps her picture.

" . . . and those still to be freed . . ." Remunda is saying.

But Odelle is thinking of yet another dream. She was a trained elephant moving logs. Having been imported from Sri Lanka, she was more nimble than the other elephants around her. She was more nimble and supple and darker than the African elephants.

Here, though, she did not move logs as work but as show. When she moved a log or raised one, there were applauding crowds. She ignored them. She concentrated on the task of moving logs. The applause sounded more like murmurs and rustles than applause.

She challenged one of the African elephants to a race. Big, lumbering, wooden, they danced instead of raced. She complained that they did not know the difference between a dance and a race. One of the African elephants, though, did not join in the dance. He stood near her.

"What are you doing?" she asked.

"I like you," he replied.

They became friends. He encircled his trunk with hers. "You can tell elephants by their people," he observed. Behind them, the crowd roared.

"This circus was made for you," he said. She couldn't tell if it was flattery or not.

". . . . . ."

"What?"

"I was asking, 'Where you been, Love?'"

"What?"

"The guerrillas, I was telling you . . ."

"What?"

"Didn't want their pictures taken. They confiscated my camera. We were in the mountains. There was the sound of artillery. I pretended I hadn't been trying to photograph them anyway but the road of fallen trees."

Odelle sits on a bench in the Kew Gardens holding her filmless camera. An Englishman comes up to her and says, "Trouble you for a light?"

She blinks, not knowing what he means for a moment. Then she realizes that he's holding out a cigarette.

"No, I don't smoke," she says.

He walks off, holding his cigarette out toward others. She raises the camera and snaps his picture.

"I've always envied you; do you know that?" Remunda had said.

She tried to remember the year. What year was the filmless camera invented? What year did she photograph Remunda?

"Envied me?" asked Odelle. "I've always envied you, your photographs . . ."

"Oh, I don't mean your photographs," said Remunda. "I mean, your nerve. Taking pictures like that when there's so much going on in the world. Taking pictures like that, with all that's going on in the world."

"I've always envied your nerve too," said Odelle. But felt no need to explain.

Remunda looked as if she couldn't decide whether it was a compliment or not. Then she raised the camera and took Odelle's picture too.

"Send me a print, will you, Love?" she said.

She mused for a moment, then looked up at Odelle, her eyes large and dark. Odelle noticed for the first time how far apart they were, like her own.

"They gave me such a hassle, my love, you wouldn't believe," said Remunda.

SOPHIA

A novella

I didn't get a good look at him, but I knew that he'd been following me. Now he was sitting in the hotel lobby, hidden behind the pages of a Spanish newspaper, *El Pais*. It wasn't really a hotel, though. At one time it had been a castle. The castle, dating from the time of the Reconquest, had been converted into an inn in the nineteenth century. Now its proprietor had added elevators, electric lights, and modern furniture.

I knew the man was following me. And I knew I wasn't in the first stages of paranoid psychosis, either. I understood the signs of that. A girlfriend of mine in college had been paranoid. We were on the same rowing team. The girl's name was Laura Turk. (I love that name.) Anyway, she'd thought all sorts of people were spying on her, from the college president down to the cooks and gardeners.

And of course all of our classmates were spies, even me. "Even me?" I'd asked her once.

"Especially you," she'd said. "Especially you, Sophia." Curiously, she liked me, spy or not.

One night, though, she stole one of the boats and took off down the Thames. The Thames in Connecticut, not England. The college security people caught up with her before she did any real harm—to herself or the boat. (I think they were more concerned about the boat.) I remember when they brought her back. She was wet and dripping and wrapped in a towel and waving at me from the college security police's car and looking triumphant.

Anyway, Laura left college in her sophomore year. After that, I lost track of her. But I heard at a class reunion that she was on the proper medication, had even gotten married, and was working in New York City for the telephone company.

I do remember that once a woman by the name of Laura Turk wrote a letter to the editor of *Essence* magazine. I'm sure it was the same Laura Turk. The letter had commended the magazine for its special issue on Black love but had blasted the absurd views—what she considered the absurd views—of one of its contributors:

> Dear *Essence*:
>
> I wouldn't have Dr. ___ for my psychiatrist for anything. I'm afraid she'd consider my love for my boyfriend a delusion, or mythology.
>
> Yours sincerely, laura turk

And she'd signed her name in small letters. That read like something Laura would do.

Anyway, I wrote to *Essence* asking whether they could give me the address of that Laura Turk, but I received no reply. Perhaps it was against their policy. I kept wondering, though, whether the boyfriend mentioned in the letter was the same one that Laura had married.

Then the first time I saw Whoopi Goldberg, I thought that Laura Turk had changed her name and moved to Hollywood. But Laura was a little taller than Whoopi, and although she had the same complexion, her hair was sandy and her eyes hazel. But it was a strange hazel. Sometimes her eyes looked light brown. Other times they looked the deepest brown I'd ever seen. Made me wonder if paranoia made eyes change color.

I've come to Spain, to Madrid, not to escape a bad marriage, as the rumor has it. (It surprised me that my own marriage was what I'd once overheard another marriage called: "rumor-ridden.") I've come here to give myself some space, some breathing space, some elbow room. I love my husband. But it's rather like a movie I once saw. I can't remember the name of the movie, only the lead players: Ida Lupino, George Raft, Ann Sheridan, and Humphrey Bogart.

George Raft, standing at Ann Sheridan's door, had just kissed her and she'd pulled away.

"Don't you love me anymore?" he'd asked.

"Of course, I do," she replied. "But I still need to breathe."

The lines had stuck with me. But I hadn't used those same lines myself. Instead, I told my husband that I needed elbow room. First I took the train to New York, then I'd flown to Lisbon, then to Madrid.

While I was in New York, I went to the Metropolitan Museum of Art. They'd advertised a show dealing with Mexico: *Mexico: Splendors of Thirty Centuries*. On exhibit were four hundred works of art dating from pre-Columbian times to the present. There were works by Tamayo, Siquieros, Rivera, Orozco, and others. And there was a special series called "Women in Mexico" with about a hundred paintings, drawings, photographs, and collages by contemporary Mexican women artists.

I'd happened to hear about the exhibit while I was on the train. The woman who sat beside me had opened a brochure. I'd peeked at it from the corner of my eye and saw "Mexico: A Work of Art." Then I started jotting down addresses as the train bounded into the station.

I'd planned to spend a couple of days in the city anyway and had already booked a hotel. But instead of going to one of the shows as I'd planned (I'd tried to look up Laura Turk in the telephone directory, but if she was listed, it was under her husband's name), I took a cab to the Metropolitan and then to the International Center of Photography for the show called *Between Worlds: Contemporary Mexican Photography*.

All throughout the city there were food and films and poetry and theater and dance and music. I don't know what had inspired the city's sudden interest in Mexico, but for me, I'd spent some time in Mexico when I was younger and in many ways it was a splendid time. In fact, several of the artists who had exhibitions I'd known when they were still students at the University of Mexico. I hadn't been a student in Mexico myself, but I'd frequented a number of the cafés where students went. I didn't spend much time in Mexico City, though. I just came in sometimes from rural Mexico to see a film or to attend a lecture.

I remember once I went with a group of students to hear a lecture by the expatriate writer Margaret Randall—you know, the one who wrote *Cuban Women Now* and *Sandino's Daughters*. She hadn't written those books yet, though. I had a copy of *So many rooms has a house, but one roof* to be autographed. Randall read some poems in Spanish and talked about art and politics.

Afterwards, in a café, the students argued about her. Some of them called her an "enlightened gringa." Others felt "a gringa was a gringa." Me, well, they considered me an honorary Mexicana. I don't know what had won them over, though. I remember once when they were talking about Mexico as if it were a monolith, I had told them that they were making the same mistake that the "Black revolutionaries" were making.

"There are many Mexicos," I said.

They looked at me, then someone, probably Gabriela, applauded.

And if anyone mentioned Don Alfonso Caso or Vicente Lombardo Toledano, I knew who they meant. At least, in those days I knew who they meant. And I knew that Guadalupe Victoria wasn't just some woman on the Avenida but Mexico's first president. Guadalupe could be a man's name too. And I knew such items of Mexican history that even they themselves didn't know—and maybe didn't even care to know. Like about Squadron 201, Mexico's World War II aviators stationed in the Philippines. I remember years later at a cocktail party I mentioned them and someone—a gringa—said, tapping me on the shoulder, "My dear, you'd be good at Trivial Pursuit."

And often one of them would spot me in one of the bookstores replenishing my poster collection: posters of Emiliano Zapata or Pancho Villa or someone from one new revolutionary party or another. It was Gabriela who gave me an old poster from the USA's World War II bracero program, enticing Mexicans to come and work in the USA.

And then perhaps I was an honorary Mexicana because I always had a ready store of revolutionary quotations that they found useful for their manifestos, quotes from President Sukarno of Indonesia or Manuel Quezon of the Philippines:

> "To President Roosevelt's Four Freedoms I add a fifth: the freedom to be free!"
>
> "A nation engaged in surviving must take help from all sides, accept whatever is useful, and throw away the rest."
>
> "She gives bounty and plenty only when she's afraid." (It meant the USA; they loved that one.)
>
> "It is better to go to hell without America than to go to heaven with her!"

When I told them that one, a *gringita* sitting at a nearby table chewing a tortilla, overheard me, put her tortilla down, mumbled something in broken Spanish, and stormed out.

This amused the group. They chortled. One of them called after her, "Polvos de arroz," which means "Rice powder." She was so fair-complexioned it looked as if she'd been dusted with rice powder. But her cheeks were as pink as a cotton rose. They turned deep red when she blushed.

Or perhaps I was an honorary Mexicana for some very simple reason: I never drank Coca-Cola, the drink they associated with imperialist America. I drank only Mexican beer—Carta Blanca—or sometimes pulque, which was made from the fermented juice of the maguey cactus and which they associated with the masses, the *muchedumbre*.

I still remember all their names. Besides Gabriela, there was Adalberto, Zea, Haim, Guillermo, Maria, Velazquez, Jaime, Salvador, Izucar. The café they frequented was located on a crowded, tumultuous boulevard. Haim had dubbed it Café Everybody—"El café de todo el mundo"—because you could find every kind of person in there.

Social awareness, Haim had said once, turned people into either debaters or activists. Me, I guess, it turned into a listener. I wasn't a debater. However, in those days, I most often found myself in groups of debaters. In such groups, I was generally a listener but the sort of listener who always had the ready word or ready piece of information the others were searching for.

In those days, I liked being in the company of such people: Passionate youths who pounded their fists on the table, ranting of changing and saving the world. Angry young men and women. In those days, it was a virtue to be angry. As for myself, I could only imagine changing or saving small portions of the world, not the whole thing.

Perhaps it was my ready bits of information that won them over. Perhaps they mistook these addendums for bursts of inspiration. Anyway, after the first few times, whenever I'd incline my head and lean forward, everyone would look at me. I liked that. I mean, being able to give them some apt detail or quotation.

It was funny, though. I guess it's the same everywhere. The group would sit around the tables and talk fervently about the masses, the *muchedumbre*, but whenever I'd bring actual members of the *muchedumbre* into the group, although they admitted them . . . Well, you know that story. . . . Although they admitted them initially, they always ended up ridiculing their lack of polish or finding laughable or uncultivated or childish something they had to say or do.

That was the fate of Jicote, an Indian from one of the rural villages. Jicote's father, who was a blacksmith, had come to the city to make his fortune. But in the city, there was no need for blacksmiths, so he'd ended up working as a janitor in a high-rise office building. Still, he preferred that to working in one of the sweatshops. But he hoped to get a university education for his son Jicote, so maybe he'd become an engineer.

Jicote called the group "*pollos*."

They were the same *pollos* who once had robbed his family of their land. Because his family couldn't prove they owned it, the *pollos* had just robbed it. I'd often run across that same story again and again among rural Mexican families. Especially among Indians and mestizos. They only knew the trees and streams and hills had always been in their families, but they didn't have the notarized papers. And if they did have the notarized papers, why, they'd never been "properly notarized" the authorities would tell them, or some other legal jargon. It was the same everywhere.

Anyway, after a while Jicote stopped coming to the group. But occasionally I'd see him in the Café Everybody with a cup of espresso and a newspaper or a textbook. I wouldn't leave the group and go join him unless he was sitting with someone else or a group of others. When he just had a girl with him, I wouldn't go over.

And the same thing had happened when I brought Joaquina into the group. Joaquina's father—the group claimed—was a smuggler. He smuggled exotic Mexican wildlife across the border into the States. Parrots, macaws, sea turtles, cactus, stuff like that. These were things that couldn't be found anywhere else but Mexico. These rare things natural history museums and the collectors in the States paid fortunes for. Of course, Joaquina's father only got a few pesos for them. The middlemen got the fortunes.

I knew it was true that Joaquina's father was a smuggler. I myself had bought one of the cactus plants from him. Although I hadn't paid a fortune for it, I'd given him more than a few pesos. I never confessed to the group that I knew or that I'd purchased anything from him.

With the money Joaquina's father got from his smuggling activities, he was sending her to the university so that she could become a lawyer. Like Jicote, Joaquina eventually left the group, calling them something untranslatable.

Sometimes after, though, I saw Jicote and Joaquina sitting together drinking hot cups of cacao, the two of them sitting at one of the Café Everybody's tables and spangled in sunlight. I hadn't meant to, but I couldn't help but feel a tinge of jealousy that I wasn't the girl there with Jicote. I watched Jicote lift the hot cup to his lips and noticed for the first time how handsome, how golden he was and how beautiful Joaquina. And they both had that sort of glow that couples have when they're in love.

And so, I brought others into the group, but the same thing happened to them. Concha, Mauricio, Epfania—a Black Cuban who'd immigrated to Mexico—Hector, Zampano, and Nayara, another young Indian, like Jicote, come to the city, which was still for many in the rural parts "the promised land." The ones who stayed in the group, who were not chased out or who left of their own accord, were the original members of the group anyway. Their great grandfathers and grandfathers had all fought in the Revolution of 1910, but their own fathers were mostly upper-middle-class businessmen, university professors, architects, film directors, diplomats, and the like.

Only Haim could be what you'd call a true aristocrat. Instead of staying in Mexico, his family had lived in Europe throughout the revolution, in Paris and Berlin and Amsterdam and Madrid, returning to Mexico only during the years of Miguel Valdés, president of the aristocrats, president of people like themselves.

But the children of servants, even civil servants, prostitutes, laborers, all the lower working classes—including a fire-eater in a carnival—shopkeepers, railroad workers, oil workers, horse trainers, mechanics, even Nayara, the watchmaker's daughter, even Nayara whose grandfather was a "*vate*" or a seer, all these from the poorer sections of Mexico City, from the barrios, from Nonoalco, from La Merced, from La Palma, all these eventually drifted away from the group.

Although I too was from the lower classes, I guess it was my "foreignness" that softened the fact of my lower-class origins. Any lack of polish, I guess they attributed to my foreignness rather than to my class. Anyway, like I said, the core of the group was always praising the lower classes in their manifestos, pamphlets, and periodicals. And they wrote poetry about them, the people from the bottom, and they'd read these poems in cafés and at gatherings held at each other's houses. But when they actually met the individual, real people, they always discovered one complaint or another about them or their actions or their ideas. It was the same everywhere. The complaints weren't vicious, but they were still complaints.

Those who won favor with the group somehow always seemed to have families who'd made their fortunes in mining, as the owners, or in land speculation or cattle, the large haciendas, or in banking, in railroads, in iron and steel mills, again as owners, in sugar mills, in manufacturing, owners, owners,

owners, owners, although it didn't matter what they produced: paper, textiles, leather goods, soap, explosives, cigarettes, cigars, shoes. Or their fathers could be in the military, as long as they were officers and graduates of the famous Military College at Chapultepec, which was known as Mexico's West Point.

But poor? Well, it was okay if they were the poor descendants of an artist or a journalist. One, for example, was descended from one of the journalists who'd been imprisoned for criticizing Porfirio Díaz and for writing anti-reelection editorials. Bravo! But they loved the children of those in the professions—lawyers, pharmacists, dentists, university professors—as long as they didn't aspire to be those things themselves.

But I must confess, I liked the group immensely. But I liked Jicote and Concha and the others too. Haim and Gabriela. But still the group reminded me of that character in Chekhov's "Gusev." You know the one. Not Gusev but the other fellow. The one who was always talking about humanity, as an abstraction, you know, but had contempt for individual people. Gusev, on the other hand, never talked about humanity, but his thoughts were always about individual people.

There were only four women in the group, that is, who stood as firm members. Maria, Gabriela, Zea, and myself. The men had nicknames for us, though. Maria, they called "The Beauty." Gabriela was "The Mexican Thinker." Sometimes they called Gabriela "The Wolf." This was because of Haim, who was a great fan of Hesse's, and like Harry Haller, he said, she had "wild, shy" eyes. And Gabriela drank brandy, but it had to be Mexican brandy, or she'd drink sangria. As for Zea, they called her "The Glance," because they thought she was a great flirt, despite being what Haim called the most politically astute among us. Sometimes they referred to Zea as "The Virgin," we found out, for although she was a great flirt, she was still one.

As for me, they referred to me as "The Little Quijote." Again, it was Haim's name for me. "The Mysterious One" they'd tried to call me at first, but after they got to know me, it was Haim who renamed me.

The women never called the men nicknames to their faces.

Behind their backs, though, we had various names for them: Rooster, Snail, Pea, Penguin. Never anything abstract or philosophical. Except for Haim. Haim had a companion nickname to Gabriela's. We called him "The Mexican Thinker" too. She then was "La Pensadora Mexicana" while he was "El Pensador Mexicano." Occasionally we called him a wolf too, but to his face.

Let me tell you about Haim. Haim considered himself "pure Mexican," dating his ancestors back to the Olmecs, the ancients, as he called them, the original people. But his ancestors were also the conquistadors, and Gabriela confided once that one of his ancestors was also among the Confederates who'd settled in Mexico after the Civil War in the States. After they were defeated by the Union Army, they'd left the States and traveled to Mexico and settled in a town called Carlota, where they tried to create a New Virginia for themselves. Although most of the Confederates eventually returned to the States, Haim's ancestors had stayed in Mexico and had blended into one of the old Mexican families.

Curiously, though, it was Haim, who, when we were once all sitting in the Café Everybody, cornered me and said how he could see the Olmecs in my face. Then he started talking to me about Africa. He could see Africa in my face too. He was high from pulque and he was telling me about the fugitive slaves. I'd always known about the slaves escaping north to Canada, but did I know about those who'd escaped south to Mexico and settled in places like Veracruz?

I told him I didn't.

He started telling me about Black slaves escaping from the US plantations and from slave ships and settling in

Mexico, and of course, he said, the Spaniards, the conquerors, brought along with them their African slaves to the colony. New Spain, it was called in those days, he said, not Mexico.

All the time he was talking I could see Gabriela eyeing us, but she didn't bend an ear to hear what we were saying. She and Adalberto were scribbling on a pad something to go into a new manifesto.

"Do you know when slavery was abolished here?" he asked. I admitted that I'd never thought about it.

"1829. And without bloodshed." He put his finger to his lips and whispered through his finger. "Without military action. Only the gringos in Texas put up any protests."

Although Texas was still part of Mexico then, there were still many gringos, he said. Northern Mexico was sparsely populated, and so the stupid Mexican government had recruited them to come fill her up.

"But to be descended from Africans in Mexico is not the same as in the States, you see. Jose Maria Morelos, the liberator, you see, was descended from both Blacks and Indians. And Naga, do you know Naga?"

He fingered my collar. I admitted that I didn't. I glanced at Gabriela, but she was scribbling something.

"Naga, the cimarron, was a Congolese." He leaned forward and whispered into my ear again. "He escaped from his Portuguese masters and came to Veracruz."

I held my napkin to my nose to avoid the strong smell of pulque.

"What are you boring her with?" asked Gabriela.

Haim took another swallow of the pulque and laughed at her, then he leaned back into my ear and whispered the name Yanga.

I said nothing.

"Yanga, the rebel," he said.

"We should all study Yanga. Do we talk of guerrilla strategies? Why, Yanga used guerrilla strategies in resisting the Spaniards and he was more successful. Why, he was more successful than any of the other slave revolutionaries anywhere. Not just slave revolutionaries. Yes, we should all study Yanga, my dear. The Spaniards never defeated Yanga."

He slumped across the table and slept. Later, back in the States, I read up on Yanga and found out that the Spaniards hadn't defeated Yanga not because Yanga had defeated them instead, but because the battle had ended in a draw, a standoff, so the Spaniards agreed to a treaty with Yanga and his followers. I was disillusioned when I learned the terms of the treaty. In order to keep their freedom, Yanga and the other guerrillas had to "forswear violence," agree to stop being troublemakers, and, not only that, they had to help the Spaniards hunt other fugitives and return them to slavery.

Haim must have thought he'd told me all that, for when he woke up from his pulque sleep, he looked around at everyone, then winked at me. "It's enough to disillusion you, isn't it?" he asked.

Everyone was still sitting at the table. Gabriela gave him her shy, wild stare, and he started telling me where I could find the present-day descendants of those Africans: "San Lorenzo, San Nicolas, Cuijla, Valerio, Trujano, Veracruz, Acapulco."

". . . y otros pueblos negros . . ."

I got up and went to the bathroom. When I came back, he was still talking, although I don't even know if he'd noticed that I'd excused myself and gone to the bathroom.

"In some of the small villages, the houses are built round, like the round huts in Africa, and there are many thatch-roofed casitas. But you probably already know about the casitas. Yes? You and your Peace Co-op people. Have you crawled into one of those casitas yet?"

I didn't answer.

"Don't go to Veracruz or Acapulco; they're tourist traps. I advise one of the smaller villages."

He took his finger and traced the side of my jaw. "I see Olmecs right there." Gabriela eyed us.

I wanted to ask Haim whether these villagers thought of themselves as Mexicans or descendants of Africa or both, but he took another pulque sleep, and Gabriela was still eyeing us.

That night I stayed over in the city in one of Mexico's youth hotels. But I dreamed that I got lost in one of the villages that Haim had talked about, one of the "*pueblos negros*." The people were all dark-complexioned like myself and quite friendly to me. I'd been on my way to some other village, driving south in my jeep from Mexico City, but had found myself in that one.

The people did a dance for me, a dance in which they wore masks and then another dance that could have only come from Africa. Its gyrations resembled some sort of fertility dance. I remember, even in the dream, that I felt slightly embarrassed watching it, although the women when they were dancing behaved quite modestly, almost bashfully.

I asked one of the women the name of the dance. "Jarabegatuno," she replied.

Oddly enough, years later, I came across the name of such a dance. I must have read of it somewhere and remembered it inside the dream.

These villagers didn't pronounce Spanish the way Haim and Gabriela did but said "*poque*" for "*porque*," "*pa*" for "*para*," "*sena*" for "*senora*," "*jablar*" for "*hablar*," and instead of calling the tallest man in the village "*muy grande*," they called him "*grandotote*."

I watched as the women sat in front of their thatch-roofed casitas weaving straw hats, while the men of the village tilled the fields, growing corn, beans, and squash, and pruning their fruit orchards.

It was like an African village, with the tasks of men and women divided. For instance, the women kept the seeds and gathered roots and nuts for food and medicine. They raised chickens and gathered shellfish along the riverbanks. Only the men were allowed to fish or make small boats.

Some of the villagers had round faces. Olmec faces. Others had faces that reminded me of jaguars with their slanted, almond eyes and protruding lower jaws. I kept waiting for them to turn into jaguars, the kind of transformations that occur in dreams, but they stayed human.

The village architecture was full of curvilinear and rounded designs, rather than sharp angles. Again, very African. I watched as the artisans worked, never measuring anything. While the statues they made were disproportionate or nonsymmetrical, still they seemed somehow perfect.

Only the men, one of the women making a straw hat informed me, were allowed to make sculptures or do architectural work.

Women's art, she said, could only be expressed in woven things. It was also the women who put the thatched roofs onto the casitas once the men had finished making them. Both men and women, however, were allowed to tell stories. Children could tell stories too, except children's tales should contain no proverbs. Only grown-ups, who had wisdom, could use proverbs. The older the grown-ups, the more proverbs were allowed. An old man or old woman's story could be a string of proverbs.

It didn't take me a long time to learn all these things in the dream. I learned them instantly. I went to one of the old women.

"What's your name?" I asked her.

"Shaguaripas," she laughed, then turned into Gabriela eyeing me with her wild, shy eyes.

She put the straw hat on her head.

"Tell me about your Mexican ancestor," she said. She laughed at me and pointed a finger. "Tell me about the woman. Why did she settle among *los negros*? Do you think we're kin?"

"Si es posible. Es una posibilidad."

The tallest man in the village, jaguar-faced, turned not into a jaguar but into Haim. He too laughed at me and pointed his finger. Then he beckoned me into one of the thatched casitas.

I woke up and when I slept again, I was in a jeep headed toward Cholula. Haim, on the seat beside me, had a lap full of straw hats that he planned to sell there.

"You thought we thought our village was the whole world, eh? Why, I've been to Mexico City and Veracruz, and even Cholula. I've even been to the Holy City. Eh?"

From the seat behind, Gabriela tapped me on my shoulder, and I woke.

Originally Haim and Gabriela and the group had referred to themselves as "The Extraordinary Ones." Then they began calling themselves simply "The Real People." Then, at the suggestion from Gabriela, they called themselves "The Real Men and Women." When Nayara left the group, though, she told me, "They might call themselves the real people, but there's nothing real about them. I'm more real than they are. And so are you."

She'd wanted me to quit the group, but I hadn't. I liked them, and they treated me like a real person. What do I mean to say?

When I was with them, I suppose, for the first time I felt like a real person. When I was with Nayara and Jicote and Concha and the others, I felt real too. I liked both groups. I liked being able to be accepted as real with them both, as "authentic." I liked moving freely between both groups and feeling authentic with them both. Los de arriba y los de abajo. The ones on the top and the ones at the bottom.

Neither made me feel like an outsider. And I liked not having to choose between them. I thought again of the Mexican ancestor, whom I'd never told the group about, who'd come to the States and settled among *los negros*. Had they made her feel like a real person? I had never known her. Una bisabuela—la abuela de mi padre. I had wanted to explore her country.

The next day when I came into the Café Everybody, Gabriela made sure I sat next to her. As soon as I came in, she grabbed my arm and sat me down beside her. She read the manifesto that she and Adalberto had worked on. (Anyway, Haim had the look of someone with a hangover.)

> The task of the Real Men and the Real Women is multifold: to untangle the meaning and the reality of Mexico, to help Mexico see herself as she really is now and as she really has been, to help Mexico understand her relationship with other nations and with herself, to help Mexicans understand their relationship with other nations and with themselves, to help Mexico in what she would and should and must become.
>
> To accomplish this, we will celebrate those at the bottom, whom we consider to be the real Mexicans. Our motto is a saying of Benito Juárez: "Respect for the rights of others is peace."
>
> We consider ourselves not judges of Mexico but her guides and seers. Whenever we speak of Mexico we say such words as could be, would be, might do this or that might well do this or that. We should say it is possible that Mexico, like any other land, is a land of possibility.

"Yes," I said.

"Yes?" she asked.

"Yes," I repeated.

Gabriela arched an eyebrow and looked at me, then she grabbed me by the arm and grabbed Haim by the other and drove us both to her villa on the outskirts of Mexico City. It was a mansion really, the kind they call Churrigueresque, a sort of rococo style.

Yes, as I have said, though their grandparents had been revolutionaries or at least considered themselves radical liberals, their parents were mostly conservatives. Gabriela kept repeating this fact to me. Her parents, she said, would never understand such a manifesto. They would never as readily, as I did, say yes to it.

"My house is your house" is a saying in Mexico. Mi casa es su casa. Gabriela wanted to make sure it was meant.

At the Churrigueresque mansion, an old man sat on the veranda in a wicker chair. Gabriela introduced him as Grandfather Jose. "Abuelo Jose, esta es mi amiga, Sophia. Recordemos." We shook hands. We sat with him on the veranda in what looked like wicker hammocks. We talked to each other, though not to him.

Hadn't she said something about reminiscing? About what? The revolution?

I thought Gabriela would talk more politics, but she didn't. She talked about films. Movies. She said something about a new Italian film that she found "revolutionary."

"No es como cualquier otra película. Deberías verlo. Es muy revolucionario."

The old man, who'd said nothing the whole time, perked up at this, and said softly, "I, too, was a revolutionary."

The three of us looked at the old man—a broad-chested old man with slender legs.

"Yo tambien fui revolucionario," he repeated. "Si, Abuelo, si," said Gabriela.

I could see Aztec and Mayan in his mestizo features, as well as Spanish and gringo. He reminded me of Anthony

Quinn. We waited for him to say something else, but he didn't. He stared out at the yucca trees.

Gabriela told me that Grandfather Jose had indeed been a revolutionary and that her grandmother, Grandmother Maria-Guadalupe, had been a "soldadera," a soldier woman.

"During the revolution, women like my grandmother followed their husbands and lovers into battle," she explained. "Didn't they, Abuelo?"

Abuelo Jose didn't reply at first, then he scratched his chin and nodded.

"They'd cook for them and sometimes they'd fight alongside them, though not always. Not always. Not all the time. Mostly they were there as companions and lovers. They'd cook or fight or make love. Whatever was needed."

"Whatever was needed," echoed Abuelo Jose.

"But women during the revolution weren't all soldaderas," said Gabriela. "They weren't all soldaderas. Some were officers in the rebel army. Could women have become officers if there hadn't been a revolution? I think not. It was then and there that women got a taste of what freedom was."

"What is freedom?" asked Abuelo.

He looked like he was interested in the answer, but Gabriela started talking about the Italian movie again. Finally, we left the veranda and went into the courtyard.

"Some were spies and others smuggled arms from across the border, from the States," she said. "It embarrasses him when I talk about the revolution."

"Why?" I asked.

She put her finger to her lips and pouted. She nodded toward the soldadera, that is, her grandmother, Maria-Guadalupe, who was in another corner of the courtyard sitting in a wicker chair. We three sat along the edge of a fountain. A cupid in its center held a broken arrow and spouted water from its own pouty lips. I waited for Gabriela to introduce the old woman to me, but she didn't. Haim nodded to her but didn't speak. It surprised me that Haim had not said anything this whole time. Perhaps he was still hungover.

From a distance, Maria-Guadalupe didn't look old enough to have been in the revolution. But Gabriela insisted that she had been and that all of the women in her family stayed youthful looking.

"My parents are conservatives," she said. "Revolutionaries always raise conservatives. They don't even raise radical liberals."

"Don't worry, you'll raise a liberal radical," said Haim, speaking up finally.

They bantered some more. As I listened to them, I thought of what Jicote had had to say about the revolution. His own grandparents and great grandparents had much to say about it. For them, the revolution was no glory story, no romantic tale of soldiers and soldier women. Rather the villagers had feared both sides.

Neither the federals nor the rebels meant to do them any good. They'd both ride into their village big as you please, and the villagers could expect the same rape and plunder, although there were Indians in both rebel and federal armies. Rape and plunder from both sides, he repeated, from both the federals and the rebels.

"They both tried to take our land from us," he said. "They both said we didn't have the proper documentation to prove it was ours. It's the same story everywhere. Es la misma historia."

Unlike Gabriela, Jicote didn't use "pure" Spanish when he told his tale of the revolution. Instead of "*mujer*," the Spanish word for woman, he said "*chapa*." Instead of calling himself the Spanish word for Indian, "*indio*," he called himself "*naco*." There were other words he used: the word "*unji*" meant "*dulce*" or sweet, and the word "*xanti*" meant "*ebrio*" or drunk.

The angrier he got as he spoke, the more his words changed from those of standard Spanish, and he spoke words in a language I was not familiar with, and even in Spanish used the familiar form with me like we'd always been old friends. Instead of "*usted,*" he said "*tu.*" "*Vos sepas,*" he would say, using the subjunctive at times when the indicative should have been normally used.

"After the revolution," Gabriela was saying, as we sat in the courtyard, "they both became union organizers."

Haim yawned and leaned a hand into the water. Yes, he still looked hungover.

"They didn't have the education to take their true places as leaders of the country."

I asked her whether her parents were union organizers.

"Are you dreaming?" she asked. She was silent, then she said, "My dad's a good industrialist, and my mom's the proper daughter of an 'hidalgo.' But my grandfather, he's the one. He stays in this villa with us, but he still rides around in his second-hand Chevy and he still sometimes goes into the cantinas, and he and my grandmother, they never let the servants do anything for them, not at all, unless it's absolutely necessary. Debido a su vejez, a veces es una necesidad. It's grandfather who gave me my first pack of chewing gum and took me to my first movie."

She mused a moment, then she said, "He calls himself a revolutionary, but he's a trickster."

She pulled Haim's hand out of the water and wiped it on the hem of her skirt.

"He's very disenchanted, you know," she said softly. "Still, I think he's the only honest man. He's the only truly honest man I know. No hay hombre más honesto y honorable que él."

I waited for Haim to object and ask what about himself—wasn't he an honest and honorable man?—but he didn't question her. He leaned his hand into the water again.

And when I was standing in front of the pre-Columbian sculptures at the Metropolitan Museum in New York, I thought of Haim and Gabriela and the others. And for a moment, I thought I saw Haim at my shoulder, only to turn to face a stranger. His straight hair was parted in the middle and tied in a ponytail in the back. He looked both Mexican and Asian. He smiled at me slightly, but then a woman came and joined him. Although the woman was blonde, I could tell that she too was Latina.

I went off to view the old manuscripts and the Mixtec jewelry of gold and silver. I found myself among the paintings and stood in front of Fernando Leal's *Encampment of a Zapatista Colonel, 1921.* I imagined myself as part of the encampment. Then I wandered to another part of the exhibit. I stood for a long time in front of a Mayan whistle carved in the shape of lovers, embracing.

I left the museum and found a restaurant that was serving free Mexican beer with every Mexican meal, as part of the citywide Mexico celebration, so I ordered bean soup with tortillas and frijole pudding. Between the salt and pepper shakers was a brochure that gave a short history of Mexican beer:

> The beer we are serving is from the famous Cuauhtémoc and Moctezuma breweries. Beer was first brewed in Mexico in 1544.
>
> Since most manufactured goods in competition with Spain were against the law in "New Spain," colonial Mexicans were not allowed to make wine. Even growing vines in New Spain was against the law. Thus, while they imported their wine, they made their own beer. The Carta Blanca came from the Cervecería Cuauhtémoc brewery, established in 1890, by Jose Schneider, a Mexican of German descent.

Someone had also translated the history into Spanish:

Las cervezas que servimos vienen de las famosas cervecerías Cuauhtémoc y Moctezuma. En México la cerveza se elaboró por primera vez en 1544.

Dada la ilegalidad, en la mayoría de los casos, de competir con España en el ámbito de los productos manufacturados, a los mexicanos coloniales no se les permitió hacer el vino. Hasta el cultivo de vides en la "Nueva España" era ilegal. Así, aunque tuvieron que importar el vino pudieron hacer su propia cerveza. La Carta Blanca tiene su origen en la Cervecería Cuauhtémoc, establecida en 1890 por José Schneider, un mexicano de ascendencia alemana.

I drank the beer and thought again of the Café Everybody. For most of the group, it was probably still Mexico, 1968. I could picture them, some gray-haired now or, like myself, their hair with specks of gray, huddled together in some storefront café. Old revolutionaries. *Viejos revolucionarios.*

I still had an old photograph of all of us in the early days. We were gathered around a café table. I sat on the edge of the crowd, my hair half-kinky and half-straight. I was waiting until the straight part grew out so that I could wear an Afro, although Laura had said that washing your hair in a strong detergent took the permanent out. As for Gabriela, she was in the center of the group, with luxuriant long black hair that she held taut in her fingers. Indeed, she did have what might have been a feminine version of Harry Haller's eyes. Shy and wild.

Looking across the room at a group of middle-aged Mexican Americans, I imagined them as my group. Mine? Anyway, I tried to imagine Haim and Gabriela and Adalberto and Maria and the others with specks of gray in their hair and a few more lines in their foreheads and around the mouth. Perhaps all heavier, except for Haim, whom I imagined always tall and lean and muscular.

Although Gabriela sat in the center of the photograph, Haim's black and penetrating eyes always seemed the true center of it. Old revolutionaries. *Ancianos revolucionarios*?

But in the photograph, we all looked enchanted. Youth's enchantment. *El encanto de la juventud.* Haim now was a newspaper man, a political journalist in the capital. Adalberto was a government official. Others worked in family businesses or independently followed the careers of their fathers. Gabriela wrote books, mostly biographies, and was a member of the United Front for Women's Rights. All of her biographies were about women.

She'd written about Laura Torres, Mexico's famous militant feminist, and about María Manuela Herrera, who was said to be the mistress of Father Miguel Hidalgo, the father of Mexican independence, of Josefa (Chepa) Alvarez, the famous Yagui Indian soldadera during the revolution, and of course of Sor Juana Inés, the remarkable poet-nun and scholar.

Now I read somewhere that she was working on a biography of Sister Concepción Acevedo de la Llata, also known as Madre Conchita or Concha, and who had taken part in the Cristero Rebellion in the 1920s. Although Gabriela herself was far from boring, I'd expected her biographies to be boring. But they weren't.

They read like novels. Her articles though were mostly boring, although they dealt with a subject that interested me: social and political thought in Latin America.

She didn't write anything under her real name, Gabriela Chayuco, but under the name Gabriela Juárez. (In 1904, Laura Torres had founded a group called the "Admiradoras de Juárez.")

When the group of middle-aged Mexican Americans rose to leave the restaurant, one of them looked toward me and smiled. Old revolutionaries. It was the same everywhere.

Well, they had allowed me to sit with them at the Café Everybody. Why had they?

Haim said I had a touch of what he called "Mexicanity." *Mexicanidad.* I reminded him, he said, of a dancer he knew from Tlatilco. Viva Mexico! Peace and bread.

I returned to the Metropolitan Museum again to stand in front of Diego Rivera's *The Billionaires*, wondering if I'd spot any of my friends from the early days. Some of their paintings were here: a landscape with jacaranda trees; then there were the more political ones: one called *Vendidos*, the sellouts. I remember the young man who painted it, one of the quieter members of the group: brown, insolent eyes, high cheekbones, hair almost as kinky as my own. He wore huaraches always and always dressed like he knew Pancho Villa dressed, in a brown wool sweater, khaki trousers, and riding boots. Even in the heat, he wore wool sweaters. Everything but the big sombrero.

I remember too that he was the only one who never ridiculed any of those lower classes whom I'd brought into the group.

Salvador. I remember once he'd said something to me.

"You not middle-class, are you?" he'd asked. "No eres una chica de media clase, verdad?"

"No," I said.

He didn't say anything for a long while, and I thought that was all that he'd intended to say. But then he told me that he regretted that he was middle class, because the middle class, he said, a middle-class person could never be a true revolutionary.

"No es posible que un verdadero revolucionario emerja de la clase media."

I disagreed with him and tried to note revolutionaries who sprang from the middle classes. In fact, I held that it was quite the opposite.

Pancho Villa, too, he said, hadn't liked middle-class revolutionaries. Middle-class revolutionaries, he said, who "always slept on soft pillows." They weren't real revolutionaries but merely revolutionary pretenders.

And he was the only one in the group who knew any Indian language. Nahuatl. At least he knew how to say "Tlen nanquitoa?" which meant "What do you say?"

And there was a painting of his here at the museum by that name and also one called *The Night of Tlatelolco*.

The artist, I learned, had been jailed during that night. It was in October 1968. I'd already returned to the States by then. But President Díaz Ordaz had sent his police forces into the Plaza de las Tres Culturas. A few students with "connections" had been released, but Salvador wasn't released until he was pardoned by the next president, Luis Echeverría, in 1971.

I stood for a long time in front of *The Night of Tlatelolco*, which resembled in some ways Picasso's *Guernica*.

He'd also done portraits of members of the Armed Revolutionary Movement and the Armed Revolutionary Forces of Pueblo while they were hiding out in the Guerrero mountains. I didn't know any of that history, though. While I'd known those young men, although their talk was radical, none of them were hiding from firing squads; they were all quite visible and in the cafés.

I asked a woman standing beside me whether she knew if the artist Salvador was in New York along with his exhibition.

"My dear, I haven't any idea. You'll have to ask the curator. The curator would know. But he's rather derivative, don't you think?"

I didn't reply.

From New York, I flew to Lisbon. Lisbon faces always reminded me of those of Mexico. I spent a few days in the oldest part of the town, called the "Alfama." There were a lot of winding, narrow streets and old restaurants where one could sit all night, drink *porto*, and listen to the fados, forceful songs based on human passions and human destiny. In most folk songs, in most countries, there is always a genuineness, or should I say "authenticity"? When folk songs are genuinely sung, there are never any false notes.

In a tiny restaurant in one of the arcades, I sat at a table next to some modern-day pilgrims. The tables were so close to each other that we might as well have been sitting at the same table, and so they began talking to me as if I were part of their group. They'd just come back from seeing the Virgin of Guadalupe in the mountains of Spain and they were on their way to the town of Fatima, Portugal. In 1917, the Holy Virgin was said to have appeared to several young shepherds there. They shared a bottle of wine with me and talked of their pilgrimage, and though I wasn't a Catholic, I had an urge to join them on it. In fact, they urged me to come along with them. They were traveling by RV and so had plenty of room.

"I'm not Catholic," I said.

"They're not Catholic either," said one of the women in a button-shouldered yellow tunic. A boyfriend jacket was draped behind her chair, and she smelled like she'd bathed in perfume. She wore a gold bracelet watch that I'd just seen in one of the shopping arcades. Her face was so bronze from her suntan that she looked as if she were wearing a tin mask, but when she talked, her features were very supple.

"Yes, I am Catholic," said a red-haired woman. She too wore a tunic, a striped and hooded one. She wore no jewelry, though, and smelled like dusting powder. Tigress. The kind I wore myself. "And I'm the only one in this group who is a real Catholic. Everyone else is a pagan. They'll all be going to Fatima just for a tourist attraction. You might as well come along. We're staying at a hotel near the sanctuary. Plenty of room. And they've got group rates, so it'll just cost you a few pennies."

I smiled at her and shook my head. She sounded like a tour guide as she described Fatima. From there they planned to go to Figueira da Foz, which was a little fishing village on the Mondego River.

We shared another bottle of wine, whose Portuguese "*vinho verde*" meant "green wine." But there was no such thing as green wine, everyone learned. You had to order either a red *vinho verde* or a white one. We ordered a red one.

One of the group, a paint salesman from Racine, Wisconsin, insisted that I should at least join them at the spa, if I didn't want to come along to Fatima. When he learned I was on my way to Spain, he asked if I'd ever been to La Toja, the Island of Health.

"When we're not doing pilgrimages, we're doing spas," he said and winked at me.

They were all of my generation, but it seemed as if they were older. I remembered reading an article once that said that most people of my generation felt estranged from their generation, or rather estranged from their chronological age. I wondered if these pilgrims felt such estrangement.

"It'll do wonders for ya," he was saying, touching my elbow.

"She don't need wonders, Nicky; lookit that skin," said one of the women. "It's like cocoa butter."

"Everyone needs wonders," said Nicky. "Come to Mondego with us."

"It ain't Mondego; it's Figueira da Foz," corrected the woman. "It's only on the mouth of the Mondego River."

"You got a mouth like the Mondego River," said Nicky.

"I'd love to, but I'm on my way to Madrid, like I said. I'm promised."

"She's promised," said the woman. "So there."

"It's Figueira da Foz," said Nicky, looking into his brochure. "So there."

"What's this dollar sign doing here?" asked the woman, staring at the bill. "I thought we paid 'em in escudos or something."

"It is escudos," said Nicky, reaching for his wallet.

"They use the dollar sign in place of the comma," I explained.

"What comma?"

"The decimal comma."

"What in the fucking world is that?"

"Pagans, didn't I tell you?"

I explained to them that while Americans used a period, Europeans used a decimal comma, and instead of a decimal comma, the Portuguese used what looked like the American dollar sign.

They all stared at me like I was some crazy woman. "But it is a dollar sign," said the woman.

"This is Europe, my dear," said Nicky. "They have funny ways."

"I know, but they're not supposed to have dollar signs in Europe. What's the sign for an escudo?"

When the waiter came, he explained it to them. I explained to them again, and an Englishman at a nearby table explained to them. I reached for the bill, looked in my purse, and put down my share of the escudos. They handed over their escudos and let the waiter decide what was what. "Isso e isso. Obrigado," said the waiter.

"La Toja," said Nicky, as I rose.

Outside, I followed the sound of another fado. "E se os pássaros esquecerem como cantar?" But instead of going inside to the new restaurant, I returned to my hotel and packed for Madrid.

I suppose the man following me is some sort of private detective my husband has hired to keep track of his crazy, errant wife. I'd seen him in the Vielas, and now in Madrid I saw him in one of those narrow streets near Cybele's Square and then again in the Rastro, the flea market. And then again when I had on my turquoise sweatsuit and my running shoes and was jogging along the Manzanares, a towel draped around my shoulders. I used to write articles on ecosystems protection and management, on restoration ecology and the ethics of ecosystems restoration, stuff like that. My husband used to co-direct a nature sanctuary in the States, before he retired. That's how we met. We were both in Tanzania for a conference on restoring Africa's ecosystems. That's as close to revolution as I ever got. Most people, though, mistake me for an aging African American entertainer, whose name they can't remember.

Like me, he's the color of mahogany, the man following me. At first, I took him for a North African, perhaps a Moroccan. But now I'm sure that he's carrying an American passport and is as African and American as myself.

He's a big man with the sort of moustache they call a walrus moustache. In the Rastro, I got a good enough look at him to know that. And to know how closely he resembles my husband. But my husband's moustache isn't so droopy. Sometimes, my husband, too, is mistaken for some other nationality. Once in New York while we were strolling near the United Nations building, he was accosted by a UN official who mistook him for a visiting North African diplomat.

He hadn't liked it at all, but I felt flattered. He grumbled. He never liked being mistaken for anything other than what he was. I remembered once being mistaken for Indonesian. I'd felt flattered.

After getting my key from the desk clerk, I turn to get a closer look at the man, but he's hidden behind the pages of the newspaper. The lines on his forehead look weary. He doesn't even try to disguise himself.

When I first saw him, I was at an outdoor festival. The table was filled with assorted seafood: oysters, crabs, lobsters, squids, and small turtle pies. Crowds jostled my shoulders as I picked up one of the turtle pies. I moved to another table that was piled just with fresh oysters. Eating them made me think of another story by Chekhov, "Oysters." About a little boy who has a nightmare about eating oysters, because you've gotta eat them alive. All the adults around him ate them alive, and only adults were allowed to eat them. His father ate them but forbade him to. I can't remember the theme of the story or what Chekhov was trying to say. Something to do with the modern world?

"Oysters! Give me some oysters!"

"Do you mean to say you eat oysters?"

When I turned, nibbling an oyster, I noticed him for the first time. He was standing against a wall and drinking from a paper cup of wine. Like I said, not even trying to disguise himself.

Up ahead the street was full of dancers. I'd gone to the festival because the desk clerk had said it was free, free for everyone.

No matter in what crowd, I can always pick him out. And he never tries to disguise himself.

SCREEN TEST

A fragment

BUTTERFLY: So, like what do you want me to do?

VOICE: Say anything . . . What's your name?

BUTTERFLY: Butterfly. I was like named after Butterfly McQueen, you know. But don't make any jokes.

VOICE: Say some more.

BUTTERFLY: Like what?

VOICE: Anything.

BUTTERFLY: Like Shelley Winters is my favorite actress. Like she's really human. You know. Like . . .

VOICE: Go on.

BUTTERFLY: Like I'm in this class where we like watch these like non-Western films, you know. Not like non-Western films, but, you know, like films not from the West?

VOICE: Yeah?

BUTTERFLY: They're like you know really interesting because you like get a different view of the world, even though they like still take a lot of their filmic techniques from like the West, you know. But like the stories, like the pace of the stories is like different, like slower, and like you get this whole different view of the world, you know. And like the other kids in the class like they'll talk about these films and like there's never anything in-between like.

VOICE: What d'you mean?

BUTTERFLY: Like either it's they'll like talk about how much they love them, or they're like finding every fault with them technically, but there's like nothing in-between, you know. There's no in-between. And then like someone always invariably says, "The actors are so full of sensuality." Always, like you know you can always count on someone to say that. Like we were like watching this Indian-from-India movie and like afterwards like this girl says, "Oh, I loved it and the actors were like all so full of sensuality."

VOICE: You're very sensual.

BUTTERFLY: These actors in this movie like they were all so beautiful you know, but like there ought to be like some way like to respond to these non-Western people's beauty without like saying "sensual," like reducing people's beauty to sensuality, you know.

VOICE: But you are very sensual.

BUTTERFLY: But like you know they'll call Sophia Loren sensual, but then like they'll call Greta Garbo like divine, you know, so like why couldn't these Indians from India like be divine, you know?

VOICE: Don't you like to be called sensual?

BUTTERFLY: Like you know like I don't have anything against sensuality, but like there ought to be a way to respond to different people's beauty with something like more than that, you know. Like this one Indian-from-India in the class like didn't have anything to say except like, "It expressed the country." The outsiders, like they were going on and on about it. But it did like express the country, you know. Like . . . should I go on?

VOICE: Please do.

BUTTERFLY: Like there was this movie with Tony Musante and like Florinda Bolkan. I believe that's her name. I know it's Florinda and like anyway they were like divorced or something and like then he like wanted her to spend a day with him in Venice or something like that. Tony Musante. I know it was him who played the man because I used to think he was like this Italian actor, but he's like American, you know, except but with Italian ancestry . . . Like I really like, like the experimental theater, you know? . . . Like to be a real actor I like think you should like watch everything you do, like even the most banal little things, like you should even like watch the way you crack an egg, you know? . . . Trivial little things like that. . . . Like how would Lady Macbeth crack an egg? Like I couldn't even imagine Othello cracking an egg, could you?

VOICE: That's fine.

BUTTERFLY: Like can I say some more?

VOICE: Go ahead.

BUTTERFLY: Like I just started thinking about this other movie, you know. Like in the beginning of it they were like the victims, you know, like taking shit, like getting their asses kicked every which way, you know . . .

VOICE: Uh . . .

BUTTERFLY: Let me go on. So like and then in the middle of the movie they like got in the position where they could be like the ass kickers, you know, and so like everybody cheered them on, you know, and they really kicked some ass. Like it was really funny.

VOICE: I bet it was.

BUTTERFLY: Like it's funny how when it's your ass they're kicking, they don't care how much ass they kick, but then when it's your turn to kick their ass, they start talking about like "Hey, wait a minute, that's too much ass." Like, you know what I mean? Like, a little is okay. Like, you know. Then they like suddenly discover there is a thing like called too much ass, you know . . . Like I like liked it seeing the other asses getting kicked for a change. It was like you wished you could get up there, like climb up there on the screen and like and like kick some ass with them, you know. Like they didn't even notice that like there was some ass getting kicked till it was like their ass, you know . . . It was a nice movie, but I like thought basically it was like celebrating like decadence, you know? Like I wouldn't like want to perform in a movie that celebrated decadence, no like I'm discussing another movie now, like, you know, the audience doesn't like know when you're like just presenting decadence and like celebrating it, you know. . . .

VOICE: Tell us your name again.

BUTTERFLY: It's like Butterfly, you know. Like I was like named after Butterfly McQueen, you know. Like there are a lot of people who like don't even know like who Butterfly McQueen is, like. I mean like they think I mean the queen butterfly, but like butterflies don't have any queen, like that's the bees, you know. It's funny how otherwise intelligent people have these little gaps in their education, like things you'd expect them to know because like nearly everyone else knows, like this gap in my teeth, but that's like supposed to make you more sensuous, being gap-toothed, I mean . . . But I really knew I like wanted to be an actress the time I wanted to climb upon that screen . . .

A SPY STORY

I drive up the Connecticut coast to a farmhouse. Fog, fern, a corral for horses. I first met the woman when I was a college freshman and she was the mistress of a girlfriend's older brother. She's a private detective born in Abidjan, in Ivory Coast, but I've heard rumors that during the Algerian War in the mid-1950s (she didn't look old enough for that) she was a spy living in Paris, pretending to be a student at the Sorbonne. I don't know, though, if she was a spy for the French or for the Algerians.

Before the war she'd had both French and Algerian friends. She was friends with the sons and daughters of petit French government officials, but she was said, though, to have known Messali Hadj when he was in exile in France and to have had friends who were members of the National Liberation Front. It was also rumored that she'd been deported from France in the early 1960s, and I assumed it was because of her friendships with the Algerians or because she'd favored the "rebels'" cause. It was not a rumor I would dare repeat to her, though, and in those days she pretended to be a clerk for the African Development Bank. A petite, dark-skinned, short-haired, and quite beautiful woman. Her name's Ouida.

I park my station wagon and walk up to the house. The car had almost stalled on the unpaved road leading up to the house. She'd forgotten to give me the directions, but a local auto mechanic had told me where the farm was.

We'd met on the street and she'd recognized me before I did her. The "little friend of ____'s sister," she'd called me, though I'm not exactly little now. And she's no longer ___'s mistress. And I'm no longer as timid of people.

"Salut," she exclaims as she opens the door. "Come in. Excuse the mess. I had some friends over. A polyglot of everybody. Artists, politicians, some political refugees, bankers, and a geologist I think. It was like a regular United Nations. In my business, you meet all sorts of people. I've a passion for different kinds of people. I can't get over you, you know. You've grown up."

We've only met once, but she's behaving as if we've known each other for ages.

"I remember you were such a nervous little girl. Not with me. You weren't nervous with me. But with the men."

"Je suis très confortable," I said.

"You never use '*confortable*' with a person, only a thing," she corrected.

"What should I say?"

"Je suis bien ici."

"Je suis bien ici."

I told her how when I was a child I spoke French fluently, but now there are gaps in it. As a child, one spoke a thing without knowing why one did it. As an adult, I need to know why one says a thing before I can say it.

We sat together in the kitchen, while the boy I'd come with (as we were driving up to the farmhouse, the boy had told me all the tales about her) and another man sat together in the front room near the fireplace talking. I watched her stir the goulash. No, it wasn't goulash; it was peanut stew. She told me of the dreams she used to have about food. People were always taking her plate, all the time. She'd be dished up a plate of food and people would take it. That's because when she was a girl she hadn't always known where her next meal was coming from.

My boyfriend had called her beautiful, but I hadn't thought so then.

Anyway, I'd been expecting a more exotic type of woman, and she seemed so ordinary. An ordinary little woman without even any interesting stories to tell, bantering about ordinary things while I'd expected tales of intrigue and exotic places. I couldn't even picture her in the jazz clubs, casinos, or boutiques of Paris. Did they have casinos in Paris or was that just Monte Carlo? Even the light, brown-skinned, freckle-faced, stocky man whose mistress she was seemed like any man you'd see on the street.

From my boyfriend I'd learned that she'd moved her family from a small village to the poor Treichville district of Abidjan to a villa in the Baie de Cocody district, all from her spy monies.

I sat on a stool in the kitchen wondering what the men were talking about. Us? Talk. Men talk. Women gossip.

She still has a photograph of ___, with his kinky red hair and intelligent eyes, though I know that she's no longer his mistress, that he has his wife in California.

"What is it you say you do?" she asks.

I tell her that I'm what's called a "playground design specialist," that I design and give advice on the design for playgrounds, assuring that they'll be safe for children and also that they'll give the children a broad range of play activities—for running, jumping, and building other motor skills; also for individual, creative, and group play. That kind of thing.

"When I turn up, people are always surprised I'm Black."

"Welcome to the club."

She's dished up two plates of peanut stew for us and we're sitting watching television. She's not the sort of woman I'd expect to watch TV, but there's a special National Geographic film on pygmies. Ouida leans forward, watching the film as she eats. I lean back trying not to get stains on her sofa. Small and solid furniture. Could this be the work of pygmies? And there are Indian and Asian pieces. Gifts from her "United Nations" friends? I'd just as soon have eaten in the kitchen, but she'd wanted to watch the documentary.

After the film, the host of the show talks to a pygmy woman who's written a book. The woman could be Ouida's kin, but I don't say so.

"She looks a bit like me, don't you think?" asks Ouida, matter-of-factly, glancing toward me.

"Yes, a bit," I agree, leaning forward, although I want to say that Ouida's more the beauty.

After the pygmy film there's a soap opera. I expect Ouida to turn off the TV or to change the channel, but she doesn't.

The soap opera is a continuing saga about a super-wealthy family. Ouida watches a scene intently, then she says, "I don't think she did it. If you're naive, you'll think she did it, n'est-ce pas? But she's the sort who'll stop at anything but murder. I mean, who won't stop at anything but murder. I mean, rich, beautiful, attractive people. They always have them stop at murder, though, to keep some innocence."

She straightens her napkin in her lap and lifts her plate of peanut stew. Paprika floats on top.

"Innocence or vulnerability. Maybe vulnerability's a better word than innocence."

I want to ask her whether she's ever had to . . . when she was a spy during the Algerian war, or now, as a private investigator, but murmuring something about having forgotten the bread, she goes out and comes back carrying a French loaf and a dish of golden butter.

"Relax," she tells me, as she cuts me a slice. Then she laughs.

"What?" I ask.

"Vas y, je t'ecoute," she says. "What is it you want to ask me? My ears are tiny, but I've heard just about everything."

GARLIC BREAD

A novella

I drove to New London, Connecticut, Chevalier's freshman year when he got kicked out of the Coast Guard Academy for an act of insubordination. Refusing to obey orders, some minor order, but he'd piled up enough of them. I'd been surprised when Chevalier had wanted to go to the academy (he'd claimed it was on account of the discipline), but I wasn't surprised that they'd kicked him out. We got his things together and loaded them in the trunk of my car, then we drove down the hill to an Italian restaurant and sat across from each other. Chevalier was growing a goatee and his hair was sort of longish, reminding me of the kids in the '60s.

They'd kicked him out of the Coast Guard Academy, but I was trying to convince him to get kicked no further than across the street to Connecticut College. When I was his age it had been Connecticut College for Women, but now it was coeducational. I wrote down the name of the dean that he should go talk to. "One of your girlfriends?" he asked. No, I told him she was the friend of a friend of a girlfriend. He took the name glumly and shoved it into the pocket of his T-shirt. One of his own girlfriends, I knew, went to Connecticut College. I'd never met her, but he'd sent me photographs of the two of them together. He'd first met her at some Coast Guard

Academy–Connecticut College freshman dance. The first picture he'd sent of them together she had this "nice-girl" look; in the second photograph, taken several months later, she was wearing dreadlocks and looking like somebody's "wild child."

He said nothing while I tried to convince him to go talk to the dean. He looked glum and pulled on his incipient goatee. I tried to remember the days not too far back when whatever I said was as "right as reason" or at least "as right as radar," which was a verbal game my kids used to play.

I sat there trying to remember what was more right: reason or radar. The little rebel pulled on his almost goatee. But he wasn't so little.

"Are you on your way to the zoo?" he asked.

"The three-ring circles," I said. "Circus."

I don't know why I was nervous with my own boy. "I thought it had grown into a zoo," he said.

I said nothing. Let me explain. I'm a cartoonist. Well, I write the words that go into the bubbles, and the company I work for each year has cartoon fairs where cartoonists and would-be cartoonists would come to discuss the craft. It started out small, what the director would call three-ring circuses with him, myself, and one other cartoonist giving lectures and leading workshops. It had gotten larger and larger each year with more cartoonists and would-be cartoonists attending, so that the director had moved it to a farm in Vermont, like those retreats and colonies that other types of artists go to rather than our stuffy New York offices. I was going to drive there but got the word from the academy on Chevalier, so took a detour.

"Aren't you going to say that you're surprised at me?" he asked.

"I'm not surprised at you," I said.

Mary and Joe—Mary and I are divorced; Joe's her second husband—were going to drive up, but I told them I would. Mary had been surprised that the school had called me and not her and Joe. I'd called her. "That boy's running wild," she'd said. "Yeah, you should drive up and talk to him. He just pulled this stunt to get more attention from you, you know." (She was taking psychology classes at a local community college.) "I wouldn't call it a stunt, Mary," I said, and hung up. His counselor who called had sounded so young (it turned out his counselor was also an upperclassman), at first I thought it was one of his friends playing a prank. But no, I wasn't surprised.

"With Canapa you'd be surprised," Chevalier said.

"Yeah," I admitted. "I would."

Chevalier and Canapa. By the way, Mary named our kids; anyone with a plain-Jane name like Mary, you know, would pick Chevalier and Canapa. Chevalier I call Chevy or Bud; Canapa I call Can or Can-Can.

"She lets you lead her around by the nose, and I don't," he said.

"What?"

"I don't let you lead me around by the nose."

"Is that what this is about?" I asked.

I wasn't sure what it was about. Prank? Stunt? Maybe he was just now reacting to the divorce. Maybe it had taken him this long. Was that why he had enrolled in the Coast Guard Academy in the first place?

Because of all the other schools he'd thought of attending, from Princeton to Fisk to Berkeley, I'd given him the names of the deans or professors or someone I knew there. But the Coast Guard Academy—I didn't know anyone.

"What is this about?" I asked.

He chewed on some garlic bread and said nothing.

"So what do you think you'll do?" I asked.

"Well, I won't go to Copenhagen," he said.

Canapa was in school in Copenhagen. High school Junior Year Abroad. In my day I don't remember any high school Junior Year Abroad, only college. Anyway, she'd wanted to go to Nigeria, but I'd told her she was too young for Nigeria but that maybe her college junior year abroad she could go to Nigeria. When she was mature enough. Then I'd probably suggest Kenya or Senegal, where I had friends. But most of my African friends were disillusioned sorts, who spent as much time in self-imposed exile as in their own countries. Thcy'd no doubt lecture her on post-colonialism and mix her all up. She had to be mature for that. "The colonialists got us in one fix," one recently wrote to me. "We got ourselves in quite another." And a couple of them you could call wolves. Yeah, she'd have to be mature. "That's the woman I've been looking for," said one when I showed him a photo of Gwen, my second wife. But we were divorced too at the time. "She's a divorcee," I'd said. "I like divorcees," he said. "Especially divorcees."

Anyway, I gave Canapa the name of a Black couple I knew in Copenhagen. An anchor, I called them. Leading her around by the nose?

"Maybe I'll take off a year," he said. "I'd like to see Africa, then I was thinking of enrolling in RISD."

RISD's the Rhode Island School of Design in Providence. I didn't know anyone there, but I knew a dean and a professor at Brown, nearby. I started to jot down their names, but I didn't.

"Are you still seeing Aurora?" I asked.

"Her name's not Aurora," he said. "She's from Aurora. Aurora, Colorado."

"Oh, I see."

"You want me to drive up to the zoo with you?" he asked.

"It's two weeks," I said. "You sure you want to spend two weeks with your old man?"

"Why not?" he asked.

He tore half a piece of garlic bread and handed me the other half.

"Do you really think I try to lead Canapa around by the nose?" I asked. "I just suggested . . ."

"She always jumps at your suggestions," he said. "That's what I meant. But I know you, Pop."

I stared ahead at the road. He stared out the window. We were on a narrow, winding road. The grass and trees as you got further and further into Vermont grew greener and greener. I felt like I was driving on eggs, though. I'd almost seen the old Bud, the old Chevalier, and I didn't want to spoil that.

"How do you mean you know me?" I asked.

"You and women, I mean," he said.

Me and women? I thought about him and the girls. There was the girl from Aurora, Colorado, and the one from Dalton, Georgia, and the one from Torrance, California, and the one from Alexandria, Louisiana. I could remember where they were from but not their names. The girl from Aurora had stuck longer. There were two pictures with her instead of one. With Canapa, it was either she'd try to glue herself to a boy or she wouldn't want to have a thing to do with them.

"What about women?" I asked.

"You divorced mom when she stopped letting you lead her around by the nose."

"I didn't divorce her; she divorced me."

"And Gwen."

"What about Gwen? Don't tell me."

I could still read him sometimes. I pointed out to him an inn where Robert Frost used to stay, not that Robert Frost had anything to do with this. Maybe his walls and fences. Gwen wasn't the sort of woman who'd let you lead her around by the nose, anyway, I was thinking. Gwen tried to lead you, but not by the nose. Is that what he was going to say? Either one sort of woman or the other? Can't let the boy know you better than you know yourself.

"So what does Aurora think about you getting kicked out of the academy. I mean . . ."

"Don't be a drag, Dad," he mumbled. "Relax. Chill out. Anyway, you don't like women as they really are. You only like them as you want them to be."

I'd been thinking about how the divorce had affected the kids in matters of love. But he was still the sort of kid you'd call "disarmingly honest." But I suppose that was good.

I glared at him, though, and told him to get a haircut, like plenty of people had told me.

Mary and I had honeymooned in Africa, in Kenya, in a small house at the edge of a jungle. It was not a real jungle but a transplanted, man-made jungle or at least a man-cultivated one and which reminded me of the jungles in storybooks. From the back porch of the small house we'd rented one could sip rum colas or coconut liqueur and watch the jungle. The wildlife in it was real, but safe: no elephants, lions, rhinos, or leopards but Somali ostriches, guinea fowls, frolicsome baboons, vervet monkeys, flamingos, and several hundred species of other birds and insects. Above was a deep blue sky and beyond that real jungle. The climate was perfect, like the tropics. Mary had been surprised by the small house, which she hadn't expected to look so modern, by which she meant "European." I hadn't been surprised. We were near Nairobi, and Nairobi, after all, was an international city, though you didn't get that sense of it from American TV.

We had a friendly houseboy. Mary had wanted to be rid of him because she didn't like the idea of being waited on hand and foot by anyone. But I said that he was not a houseboy but a college student who worked summers as a houseboy to pay his tuition. So she decided to keep him, simply not letting him wait hand and foot on us.

"It would make me feel like bwana," she said.

"Only men are bwana," I said.

"Well, it would make me feel like whoever. That's why I didn't want to stay at the tree hotel."

There were too many safari groups staying at the tree hotel. "Speak of the Ugly American," she whispered.

"They're not all Americans," I said.

We rented a Toyota Land Cruiser and traveled "up-country." The houseboy, or rather the young man whose name was Kudu, was our driver/guide. I rode up front with him, while Mary rode in the back with the binoculars and dust masks, photography equipment, and books on Kenyan culture, bird and animal life. Kudu, a gourmet cook, prepared all our meals, but Mary insisted on serving them, and to Kudu too. Everything he cooked was delicious, mouth-watering. To tell the truth, I've never had such good food before or since. A young man, and though mostly African, Kudu seemed a blend of all the people who had come here—African, European, Arabian, Asiatic. He was from Rusinga Island on Lake Victoria. And he spoke perfect English. Mary hadn't expected that either. She'd had her phrasebook ready to say words to him in Gikuyu.

Leading her around by the nose? Maybe that had been true back in the States, but on our African honeymoon it was she who, once she got acclimated to the place, behaved as if she belonged there. I chatted with Kudu, who wanted to know everything about Manhattan (which I then only knew superficially) while Mary handled the itinerary.

At the Masai Mara National Reserve on the Serengeti Plain we were to watch the wildebeest migration. (There were Masai there herding cattle and goats, but I mustn't watch them like they were black rhino! I didn't know that I was looking that way. I looked away from them at a nearby baobab tree, then studied a giraffe in the distance.) Mary spied a group of whites on safari sitting down to a champagne brunch after a hot-air balloon ride.

We climbed into our Land Cruiser and were off. Kudu took us to Rusinga Island, where we met his father, a fisherman. His mother made us a dinner of Nile perch. He'd taken us off the tourist trails to a scraggy part of the island, "the image of underdevelopment," as I'd heard someone call such places, but clean with round-roofed houses. It was strange to see him on his island. The islanders seemed to treat him with a sort of reverence, and he seemed to grow taller on his island and moved about like a man feeling his own strength. He left us for a while to spend some time with a girl of his, then he returned to have the dinner of freshwater perch. After dinner, other islanders came to visit. Mary sat with the women while I sat in a circle of men, who spoke half in Gikuyu, half in English. Those who weren't fishermen worked with Kudu, on the tourist circuit. (I learned that on the island he was not called Kudu but Karenga.)

The men talked of the glory times—the "grandeur," one of them called it, and of colonialism, and then of independence. I couldn't hear what the women were speaking of, but I noticed that Mary had got to use her phrasebook.

Kudu's grandfather, I learned, had traveled out of Kenya to learn the "world's ways" but had returned and resumed his life as a fisherman.

Europe he referred to as "land of mirages." He was a quite intelligent man who sat a bit apart from the others with his grandson, the law student/houseboy who I could overhear lecturing him on the benefits of modernity.

"That's the American dream," I heard the old man say, "but what of the African dream?"

I cocked my ears in their direction to listen, but what Kudu said I couldn't hear. I did hear his grandfather clearly, though, when he said, "That's naked knowledge. Naked knowledge isn't enough."

I wanted to ask the old man what he meant but felt out of place. I watched Mary, though. Mary seemed more in tune with the rhythms of the place; she sat with the women in an easy way like she was one of them. I remember how back in the States she was withdrawn, but here she seemed to assume an outgoing nature. (I remember several years later back in the States, I showed her a picture of herself with some of the island women. She looked at the picture and at herself like she was looking not at herself but at the portrait of a woman she would have wanted to be.)

Near a volcano—Mary can tell you the name of it—we went horseback riding; then back on the mainland, we took the Land Cruiser to one of the national parks. As we rode, Mary read aloud from the book about Kenya's two-thousand-year-old history, about the natural history of the hippo, the Rothschild's giraffe, the crocodiles, zebra, gerenuk antelopes, dik-dik, elephants, hyrax, eland, cheetah, kopjes. Even the history of the basaltic cliffs and acacia trees.

At the Amboseli National Park on the border of Tanzania, there were more Masai. Again, Mary accused me of watching them the wrong way.

Kudu knew one of the young Masai men and they stood talking in Gikuyu or another language.

Mary photographed Kudu with the Masai. I didn't know whether he considered himself a cattle herder or a warrior.

We took back with us a bottle of red volcanic dust and a figure carved by one of the Akamba wood carvers.

Gwen and I had not taken a honeymoon. "Honeymoons are for first wives," she'd said. We had stayed in Manhattan. A friend of hers, a supermodel (Gwen called her), had thrown us a honeymoon party and had let us stay at her apartment while she went off to Paris to be photographed.

The apartment was one of those ultra-modern kinds, everything automatic. It looked like something out of a futureworld.

"This looks like something out of a futureworld," I told Gwen.

"No, Marty," she said. "This ain't futureworld; this is the way people live today. This is the way the other half lives."

I was expecting some robot houseboy to appear, but Gwen did all the cooking. It surprised me that she cooked better than Mary. Or rather, her meals were capable of surprising. And then she led me around by the . . .

What was Bud going to say? Balls?

"Where did you and Mary honeymoon?" she asked me.

"Kenya," I said.

She laughed, gulped her gin fizz, and called me "bwana."

THE COSTUME MAKER

I am a bird of Brazil, though I wasn't born here. The blouse I am sewing looks like a bird costume. Fulana says because I sew so well, why don't I make all our costumes for carnival? But she says that every carnival. Every carnival she tells me I should be sewing carnival costumes. This carnival we'll all be birds, she says: toucans, canaries, cardinals, and any other curious bird. But we won't all be birds of the same feather. She gives them all Brazilian names. *Tucanos*, *canários*, *brejais*, *cardenales*, *papa capim*, *jassana*, *curiós*, *chachalacas*.

Then Fulana buys me a costume book. Ernesto, who works as a tourist guide, expects this carnival to see many tourists in Brazil. But there're always many tourists in Brazil at carnival, and Ernesto, who's part African and part Tupi-Guarani Indian, always says the same thing. He's always guiding tourists. If he's a bore, then he's an industrious bore. He's very much a working man, and a clever fellow too. All the tourists these days want to see the samba schools. Samba-reggae is quite the rage in New York, they say, and so many tourists who come here, especially the New Yorkers, want Ernesto to escort them to the samba schools and sometimes even teach them how to samba.

I'm waiting for Fulana to get off work, but they have her making sandwiches. And then she's taking an English class.

She knows English as well as I do, and sometimes better, so why does she need a class for it? I'll keep your secrets if you'll keep mine. She learns such phrases as that. She calls it "the revolutionary's English class" because it's taught by a revolutionary from some revolution in some neighboring country. He teaches her not to follow anyone's instructions, not even his. He says she's his best English student, but why shouldn't she be the best English student? She speaks it all the time with me. She tells him I was born in New York, but I wasn't. I wasn't even raised there. I'm from the Midwest.

Fulana was born and raised and grew up here in Rio. Ernesto says that Fulana and I resemble each other. He says we could be twins. But everybody says so.

Everyone who sees us together asks are we twins.

Perhaps that's why we were drawn to each other. When I first came to Brazil we saw each other and greeted each other like old friends. Then we rented an apartment together in the city, and she moved out of the slums. I had come here not to be a tourist but because of the social history. I was a student of social history and especially the social history of Brazil.

Ernesto drinks too much, Fulana and I tell him. Don't drink so much she says. Nao beba tanto. Fulana thinks she's in love with him, but he's already got a girlfriend.

Uma taberneira. An innkeeper. A very large woman, somewhat older than him, with a blemish on her chin, but otherwise very pretty. And Fulana's got a boyfriend also. A handsome fellow who plays the drums when he's not playing the tambourine.

As for me, I'm unattached. But I'm always buying romance novels. And I like comic books too. When I'm not buying romance novels I'm buying comic books, the kind of illustrated books written for adults, not children. Romances never have ugly girls in them, says Fulana.

We're not ugly girls, but Fulana doesn't think we're as pretty as the other girls in the city, who are known worldwide for their great beauty. And what of the innkeeper with the blemish on her chin? She's pretty except for that blemish, says Fulana. And she reminds me of someone out of a storybook.

And I don't just read romances. Sometimes I read the literature of Black female writers, which aren't always exactly romances. And Fulana also collects such works. I have given her as a present books on Black feminist theory and African American literature and cultural studies, all the books I have by Ann duCille: *The Coupling Convention: Sex, Text and Tradition in Black Women's Fiction*, *Skin Trade*, *Black Marriage*, and *Technicolored*, about "race and representation" on television.

In the evenings, while she sits reading Professor duCille, I read the illustrated novels or my romances.

"Who's that?" she asks, peering at one of my illustrated books.

"This is by Martin Tage. He's an African American who writes dialogue for comic books and illustrated novels."

"I think he's a product of your imagination," she says, as she continues reading.

When I'm not reading what Fulana considered questionable books, I sketch out patterns for the bird costumes. *Tucanos*, *canários*, *brejais*, *cardenales*, *papa capim*, *jassana*, *curiós*, *chachalacas*.

One day Ernesto introduces me to Josefina, his girlfriend, the innkeeper. She also knows Fulana and at first thinks I'm her and declares we've already met. But Ernesto assures him I'm not Fulana but the girl from New York. I don't correct him about my origins. I know Fulana when I see her, she keeps saying. Didn't I say we could be twins?

They stand kissing each other, Ernesto and his innkeeper girlfriend, although he refers to her as a "*taberneira*." They stand kissing each other, and she's almost as tall as he is. That blemish on her chin is a birthmark, and it's shaped very much like the map of Brazil. A birthmark in the shape of Brazil. (Fulana, however, thinks it's shaped like the continent of Africa or Africa in Brazil.)

I like his girlfriend, although she still thinks I'm Fulana.

She has a recording of her drummer's drumbeats.

We listen. In the apartment next door lives the revolutionary from another country who teaches English.

"I'm going to save my money," says Fulana, "and take a vacation to New York City, your hometown."

"What are you painting?" I ask the street artist. He shows me a carnival scene. He looks like Fulana's boyfriend, but I know it's not him. Just like I know I'm not Fulana. Her boyfriend's a drummer, but he doesn't mistake his girl for a drum.

Marvelous city, it's true, that's Rio. The most marvelous city in the world, even with its blemishes. Fulana says she grew up in the slums and clawed her way out, but not too far out. Sometimes she returns there, to the people, and to visit her friends there.

Fulana makes turtle soup. Where did the turtle come from to make this soup? Where did the water come from? Sometimes we eat tuna with mango salad.

In the slums, though, she introduces me to a woman who introduces us to her children. One's a stutterer. But who wouldn't stutter in a favela like this one? What does she call him? A *tartamudo*? Something like that. The woman serves us a salad with smoked tomatoes and honey, mustard and fresh ginger. A healthy, colorful dish.

"She won't let me leave without serving food to me," says Fulana, "although she can scarcely afford it. I don't visit her often. Sometimes I'll send things. She knows it's me, but I don't tell her so."

In the kitchen where she works, I'm helping Fulana make sandwiches, so that she can leave early, so that we can go to the movies. Ernesto doesn't like to go to the slums or the movies with us.

We put pickles on the sandwiches, tomatoes, lettuce, and wild onions.

Sometimes I tell them stories of New York, but they know there's no iota of truth in what I tell them. It's the New York of my imagination.

"She's a storyteller, after all," says Fulana. "She came with ideas about us. Fantastic ideas. I have to set her straight all the time."

I didn't like the movie, but I spend all day sewing carnival costumes, and in the evening I like to go to films, even those I don't like. But I like *Cafundó*; I like *City of God*. "We've got great movies now," says Fulana. "Before the scripts were poor, but now we have great movies. See how gorgeous our cinema is." Fulana and I live on a one-way street in a small apartment. Like I said, Fulana has a boyfriend, but she's enchanted with Ernesto. He reminds her of a bird of Brazil. I, too, am a bird of Brazil, but I wasn't born here.

People are always asking me what's in the bags I carry besides groceries. I tell them they are carnival costumes. Or fabric to sew carnival costumes—silks and satins and lace—and buttons and threads and needles and thimbles. And when I'm tired of sewing? I go to see films, or I read books, romances or comic books or books by indie/independent authors and authors published by established companies. There were works by Crystal Wilkinson, Ann duCille, Kambon Obayani, Lucille Jones, Richard Ford, Mary Gaitskill, Isabel Allende, Julia Alvarez, Richard Price, Don Steele, N. Scott Momaday, and Amanda Wordlaw, among others. And I have the works of Brazilian authors. Fulana says she's heard the latter is a confabulatory author, but I say she's real, and it's her works on Brazil that inspired me to come here. "And given you mistaken ideas," she says. Besides groceries and fabrics, I have books. I take one of the books, a book by an indie author and a Vietnam War veteran called *The St. Louis Tea Company and Other Stories*, and go out into the open air on the terrace and begin to read. There are palm trees on the cover, perhaps a Vietnamese landscape. This is also a country of palm trees. I eat candied apples.

I give her a copy of Kambon Obayani's *Island of Song*.

I dream that I have a boyfriend. I give him a profession. I say that he owns a shoe-repair shop. I dream that I met him when I took my sneakers to be mended. I dream that he's always asking everyone, "Onde aperta o sapato?" "Where does the shoe pinch?" Something like that. I only wear rubber heels.

We go to a farmers' market and buy fresh vegetables and fruits. We send some to a slum in Rio.

It's second nature to me now to make costumes for carnival. I call it carnival. But Fulana calls it "*carnaval.*" I'm a self-taught maker of costumes. I sew them at our kitchen table and not in one of those sweatshops where they say "Faster! Faster!" I take my own sweet time.

I'm looking at my molar. There's a fishbone stuck in my gum. I loosen it and pull it out.

"One of my girlfriends used to be married to a detective," Fulana says.

"How did they meet?"

"She couldn't get her key in her lock and he helped her. He was following someone else and spotted her."

Fulana's full name is Fulana de Tal.

There are figs left on the plate and we're nibbling them. She talks about when she was a child and there were streetcars everywhere. Now she's watching me sew the costumes at the kitchen table. I make the costumes and she makes the masks.

"When I get hungry, I could eat everything in sight, even the costumes," she says.

Now she's meditating. She's meditating every day.

It's something the revolutionary taught her. Transcendental. "Practice makes perfect," she says.

And of the glittery costumes I make, she says, "Everything that glitters isn't gold." Then, "I love Ernesto," she confesses, "but he's already in love."

I sit on the terrace and read *Where Ignorance Is Bliss*.

It's a dream. The boyfriend of my dreams again.

He's showing me how to pull back the bow. Archery is his favorite sport.

"When Ernesto first met me, he thought I was a tramp. But I'm not so trampy as I appear to be."

We're all movie buffs. Ernesto knows some of the Brazilian actors. He grew up with some of them. Some of them clawed their way out of the slums.

Ernesto and Fulana both sit at the table watching me embroider the costumes. I make the shapes of butterflies.

They're always looking at me like I'm a foreigner and I guess I am. I must be. This is another country after all.

Fulana likes to make money but to keep her honor, too, so she mostly works in factories or waits on tables. She's studying to be a bookkeeper.

She reminds me of someone else I know. I can't remember whom.

I'm a bird from Brazil, but I wasn't born here. I could dream all day.

The costumes I am making look like birds. Fulana buys me another costume book. "I want you to make all the costumes look legendary. That's right. That's the word I mean."

Marvelous city. It's true. Rio is the most marvelous city.

"You've come here with your wild imagination," says Fulana. "Now I'm studying architecture. I want to learn how to make low-cost, accessible buildings. But they must say a lot of what the people are like . . . Good geometry . . . Techniques to occupy the space . . . I love to build things . . ."

WORKER

A fragment

I'm always imagining what people think of me. In Tijuana, in Jalisco, it is the same. Always imagining what others think. Always imagining the thoughts of others. Do you find this an amusing game? Do you have your identity papers?

I'm not an ignorant person, though perhaps in this city I appear so. In my village, everyone called me a clever girl. Maybe the most clever girl in the village. Maybe too clever for my own good. When the young men picked wives, they didn't want clever girls, not girls too clever for their own good.

I should tell you something of the history of my village, how the women fought along with the men and how the women had to be clever to escape from slavery, just like the men, and that we should all be proud that although we are Mexicans we are descended from Africa, and we are proud that escaped African slaves founded our little village, our own little freedom town. Sometimes people don't have the least idea about that and are surprised when I tell them the story. I tell them I consider myself to be Mexican and African at the same time, not one any more or better than the other. Here's a photograph of me in my village.

People who work in this factory are poor but honest.

Some of the girls think I put on airs, but I don't. But in a city like this I don't have the least idea of who I am, and I don't pry into anybody's business. I keep to myself when I'm not working. Sometimes people look at me like I'm an idiot, but in my village I'm considered a clever girl. And with a point of view. In my village there are such wonderful colors. If I were a photographer, that's the image I'd like to capture. Familiar images to me, but maybe not so familiar to anyone else. It would give me peace of mind to photograph my village.

The boss orders me to do something. He looks at me with amusement. Some people say he tries to sleep with all the girls in the place, but he hasn't tried to sleep with me. And maybe it's not the truth at all. Maybe he's an honest fellow. But some people will stick to any story. He only orders me to do this and that and the other. He's not even the first boss. He's the second boss. I've seen him get some of the girls up against the wall in the corridors; I've seen that for myself, and I'm an honest person, but me he only looks at out of the corner of his eyes. Some girls he gives a quick kiss, but me he only squints at.

Some men in my village are more handsome and more clever and more honest than him.

The noise from the factory always keeps me from sleeping. I hear the noise in my dreams. I hear the noise when I'm awake. You ask me what I do in the factory? I glue plastic parts together. Nice, clean plastic parts.

Plastic parts of all kinds of things. I follow the instructions. You must glue everything together. When you go to work there, they teach you the process. Some pieces you can put together without gluing. They form tight bonds and tight seals. I work near the back of the shop.

Then I go to the cafeteria and eat the food that gives me indigestion. Sometimes I bring my own fruit and vegetables. Freeze-dried to nibble on. I mix the freeze-dried fruits and vegetables together, mix in a few nuts and seeds, and some type of whole grain. I bring my own bagged food that doesn't give me indigestion. Sometimes I mix in coconut flakes. The boss told me once I looked like an Indian, a Hindu. He and the first boss are devising new methods to make the factory more efficient. But these new methods seem identical to the old ones. Sometimes I bring my own hard-boiled eggs and put them in baggies too. Their eggs taste like rubber.

I hear the second boss tell one of the girls she's like a magnet. But he's looking at me with impatience. He's trying to teach me the new efficient method, but it's just like the old one.

I hear him tell one of the girls he wants to take her to the nearest hotel, but she won't go with him. He calls her a very industrious girl, and very pretty, but he looks like he's still angry.

I think he's going to fire her, but he doesn't. That's only because he's not the first boss, and there's someone he has to answer to. The first boss seems to be an honest fellow, but I don't know the whole story.

In my dreams, I hear the noise and fuss of the factory workshop, and then I'm gluing plastics. And some hold together without glue. They form tight seals.

Some of the girls say their real dreams are across the border in another country.

I might return to my village where I'm considered a clever girl.

MIRABEAU

Call me pied piper woman. There I was reading the Lorca poem about the barren orange tree and the tower, and there she was with oranges painted on her leather satchel. And there I was riding on the Boston subway from Back Bay to Mass. Avenue. And so I saw this little girl, and I'm a candymaker and it was easy. I always smell like chocolate and caramel and peppermint.

"What's your name?" she asked.

I said, "Mirabeau Auvergne, like the volcanoes."

"That's a nice leather satchel," I say.

"It's not leather," she replies. "It's vegan."

A little girl, seven years old maybe, carrying that vegan satchel and a picture book of kangaroos, and I'd just come back from them, the doctors, telling me I couldn't have kids. As barren as Lorca's orange tree.

And this little nappy red-haired little Black girl reminded me of me when I was seven and that satchel with oranges reminded me of Lorca.

And so I decided, then, I'd take her home with me.

We got off on Mass. Ave. and walked toward my brownstone.

Everything's unmatched. A green, blue, brown, and purple chair at the kitchen table.

The girl sits in the purple chair. Isn't purple the color of royalty?

I fix the girl a plate of chocolate chip cookies and a glass of milk.

While she eats I'm looking out the window at another brownstone. A bird leaps from the top of the building like a diver, free-falls, and, just before it lands, takes flight. Could that be a sport of birds?

I used to do upholstery work, sew cloth into hassocks and couches. I used to stuff pillows with feathers and paint the arms of chairs with protective enamel. Once I started to invent a chair my own self, to design a kangaroo chair where you could hide things. A place for hiding things. Maybe hide a kidnapped girl inside.

Now the girl's on the sofa napping and I'm daydreaming, watching imaginary birds lined up like divers on the cliffs of some South Pacific island, ready to play the free-falling game again, to see which can come within a splinter of the ground and then soar.

I'm reading Linda Dahl's *Stormy Weather*. The music and lives of a century of jazz women. Makes you wish you were one. Got some of the best lines, like pianist Billie Pierce—the other Billie—saying, "I don't know if it was rough or not, 'cause I was rough right along with it."

I was born in Boston, "Bean Town," but my parents are from New Orleans, and sometimes I tell folks I was born there too, that place that *Time* magazine once called "brooding and flamboyant, raucous and urbane, devout and dissolute." Stokely Carmichael said, "A guerrilla studies," but I'm not a guerrilla. I heard him talk once, a speech he gave, then afterwards went to the john to relieve myself—I'd been holding myself in the whole speech—and I discovered penciled on the stall, "A gorilla studies, but he's still a gorilla."

Who wouldn't want to be born in New Orleans, though? I've got the whole city running together in my veins, they say:

Cajun, Creole, German, Irish, Italian, African, Spanish, French. And I look like it. One great uncle, they tell me, used to ride the backs of alligators in a circus or carnival show. The alligators let him ride them too, like he was some sort of river god. But that was years later, after they got acquainted. At first it was all danger.

And they asked him how come he put his fool self in danger like that? And he says, "Why not?" He used to travel all over, riding the backs of alligators.

I never wore perfume until I was thirty. Every perfume I ever smelled, smelled like trouble, and I was allergic to it; it gave me migraines, or it was just my imagination. Then once when I was thirty, I opened a bottle of perfume that smelled like sunshine, fresh air, and song. I wasn't allergic to that, and it didn't give me migraines. And I started wearing that. And when I was standing on the street corner waiting for the bus to go to work, this man comes up to me and says that I looked melon-sweet—perhaps I smelled like melons?—and said how he'd like to kidnap me, and then the bus came and I got on. I ran up the stairs of the bus.

I don't know if the times were rough or not, because I was rough right along with them.

Maybe you've seen me at the store I work at, standing at the counter, folding long strings of licorice. The licorice looks like my hair, because I wear long braids. "Is that Medusa?" a little boy in a sailor suit asked once, when he came into the shop. "Hush, no," snorted his mother, embarrassed. Then she explained in an even tone, "No, dear, that's how they wear their hair. It's quite the rage."

They've got chocolate everything where I work.

Chocolate sculpture, they call it. They've got a chocolate version of Rodin's *The Kiss*. It was me who did that one. I should tell you I'm a pretty good chocolate sculptress. I can make anything from chocolate. The boss says I'm a damn good candymaker. A damn good chocolatier. But they only want you to make what's been made; they don't want you to experiment too much. This girl comes in in a yellow Lee Cooper sweatshirt and jeans. The boy's in a plaid shirt and jeans, and together they pool their money and buy the chocolate sculpture of *The Kiss*.

I take the little girl to a sweatshirt store. Sweatshirts with all kinds of pictures and snappy statements and sayings. And the little girl spends about an hour examining sweatshirts, until she finds the one she wants: "If you liked Vietnam I, you'll love Vietnam II." I'm not sure what it means, but the little girl seems wise to it. She looks wiser than her years. And I'm thinking I don't know who's kidnapped whom.

A Chicago man came to New Orleans and spotted my great uncle riding alligators and wanted to take him around the world.

"This act's too big for Louisiana," he said. "This is a world-class act."

Then he came back later and showed my great uncle a drawing of himself on the back of a fussy crocodile.

Because the man couldn't tell the difference between a crocodile and an alligator, or whoever did the illustration for him couldn't tell the difference. Great uncle liked the picture of the crocodile, but not of himself. He said the illustrator had the crocodile looking more human than he did.

"Had the croc looking more like a human being than me."

The glasses have moons and flowers on them. The woman who owns the place is North African, Moroccan, but was born in Paris. Once she was in love with someone but didn't confess her love in time, and so he married another girl. In her spare time she grows roses and is readying one for the Salon International de la Rose. She wants to win the Prix des Nautes, or some sort of prize. I think that's the name of it. The prize allows her to get to name a rose.

She wears a peacock comb in her steel-gray hair and a dress with two splits up the sides and splashed with rainbows, birds, and flowers. Older women are dressing like that nowadays, but in those days they didn't do much of that and that made her stand out. They used to tell women in those days to dress their age. Now they can dress like any age.

Les enfants, she would call all of us youngsters. *Les enfants*.

I knew you when you were knee-high to a grasshopper.

And then she'd ask us what we'd have for dinner. She was born in Paris, but it was in Boston that I met her. She had immigrated to the States and opened a tiny restaurant there. Afro-French. The tables were so close together.

Je t'ai connu quand tu étais jusqu'aux genoux d'une sauterelle.

The boss at the shop where I make chocolate, even chocolate angels, is a nervous little man. We call him Mr. Jack. He's nervous because he's got so many people to boss around. I used to think that bosses weren't nervous people, that they liked bossing people around and were all confident. In his office he eats his lunch very fast, and even then he's got chocolate makers interrupting him asking him, "Mr. Jack, what about such and such?" Every little thing seems to make him nervous. And he's very fastidious. If there are not enough paper doilies to put the chocolates on, he gets nervous. He's got a bookkeeper and someone who handles the inventory, but he's still nervous. He doesn't even make the chocolates himself, although people say he knows as much about chocolate making as anyone in the place, and he's still nervous. He's still a nervous fellow. If I was a boss, bossing folks about, I guess I'd be nervous all the time too.

In the newspaper I'm reading, there's a picture of the little girl I've kidnapped. I buy it to read on the subway going to work, and I read it again on the subway coming back. When I unlock the door, the little girl, wanting her freedom, has trashed the place. She's trashed the whole place. Everything. And now she's watching Grace Jones on my TV. I got old tapes of her.

So I don't say anything. I sit down to read a book about a poor Black sharecropper family with three daughters. Two ignorant daughters and one smart.

Except the two ignorant daughters, says the author of the book, "are ignorant because they ignore the things that other folks take for granted that one needs to know." That's not the exact quote, but it's as close as I remember it.

"Is this me? Is this me?" asks the little girl, holding up the newspaper.

I don't answer her right away. I wonder why she doesn't recognize herself. And then I'm thinking about once on the subway I saw two men hitting each other with rolled-up newspapers. An affectionate hitting, the kind two buddies give each other. Like someone said that that was the only way that men could show affection, some sort of emotion, anyway, was by popping each other every now and then. At least in the old days.

The girl is wearing her new sweatshirt when I take her to her door. They think I've found her and want to reward me.

"You found her! You found her!" they exclaim.

And the girl doesn't say I didn't find her. She doesn't give me away.

The little girl, she's beaming like sunshine, and me, I'm maybe a moon.

At work I sculpt a chocolate alligator and I sculpt a kangaroo. Mr. Jack says I need to put a baby kangaroo—what do you call them? he asks. A joey?—in my kangaroo's pouch. He keeps repeating what I need to put in its pouch. But me, I'm not so sure.

We could at least pay you for her new clothes.

No thank you, madame et monsieur.

JIGSAW SANDALS

It was 1938, before most folks had any thoughts of war, when I started working as a ticket taker at this local Black movie house. Not a fancy one. Not one of those palace types. It used to be a silent movie theater, then Mr. McElroy got his license, bought it, and started running talkies.

Mr. McElroy is one of those light-skinned colored men. Seems like you see plenty more of them down South than you do up North. I suppose it's because of the history of the South, the Southern story. Anyhow, people say the reason they gave Mr. McElroy his license is because they thought he was a white man. Still, there are others who say he really is a white man, just pretending to be colored. And there are folks like that, passing for colored, just like there are colored folks passing for white. I think I read a story like that somewhere, about who's passing for whom. That Langston Hughes story.

Anyhow, that week we were running an all-colored movie. They say all-Black today or all–African American, but in those days, and when I was a youngster, they said "all-colored." Sometimes they would say "all-Negro." It was called *The Killers*, I think. Not from the Ernest Hemingway story. This was a different *The Killers*. I think that was the name of it. It starred Lawrence Chenault and Willor Lee Guilford. I know some Chenaults and Guilfords in this town, but I don't think they're any kin to those movie actors or have any movie stars in the family.

But you've probably heard of them, or if you haven't heard of them, you've probably seen them in the movies.

I first saw Willor Lee Guilford at the Palace Theatre in Louisville, Kentucky. They've got two Black theaters in Louisville. The Palace and the Funky Lumber. I don't know how they came by that name; the Funky Lumber, I mean. I've never been there to the Funky Lumber, but the Palace is really nice. And it does look kind of like a palace and a real tribute to movie culture. That was how they were constructing theaters in those days. That was the type of architecture, true palace-designed theaters.

Because the movie theater in those days was a fancy and fanciful thing. And people would dress up to go to the movies, unlike today.

The theater I was working in, though, wasn't a palace, like I said. But, as for me, I like to go into any movie theater and see the likes of Willor Lee Guilford on the screen and not just Paulette Goddard, Evelyn Brent, or Pola Negri, although I like Pola Negri. And ain't that a name for a woman? But I mean, women who look like us.

We also showed movies with Nina Mae McKinney and Mantan Moreland. Those all-colored-cast movies, that was my first time seeing so many of us on the movie screen and playing all kinds of roles and every type of role imaginable and playing the great roles, heroes and villains, gangsters and cops, cowboys and cowgirls, scientists and doctors even. Just use your imagination.

It was 1938, like I said, and I was twenty-one or just turned twenty-one. I was taking tickets and wearing those jigsaw sandals, you know, which were considered pretty darn stylish in those days, and being a youngster I could wear shoes like that. Nowadays, I have to wear shoes with a little more arch support in them.

As for me, I'm originally from Covington, Kentucky.

Actually, I'm from a little country town near Covington. But I was staying in Lexington, Kentucky, with my sister Alberta and her husband, Turk. Turk is from Zion's Hill, Kentucky, one of those original "freetowns" that the Blacks formed after they were emancipated. The free Blacks would form their own little towns, you know, like Warthumtown and Davistown and Little Davistown and Bracktown and a lot of towns throughout the South and out west. They live on Race Street, I mean in Lexington, my sister Alberta and her husband, Turk. When I first heard the name, I thought they were saying "Raise Street."

They don't live in one of those shotgun houses. You know, those shotgun houses. One of those straight-back little houses that they say you can shoot a shotgun through it and the bullet goes in the front door and out the back. No, they live in one of those duplexes with a family next door. Or maybe you could call it two shotgun houses tacked together. Except the rooms were kinda catercornered and not straight-back.

It's my sister Alberta who got me the job at the movie theater taking tickets. She took me right over to see the projector-man, not Mr. McElroy, because Mr. McElroy allowed the projector-man to hire the ticket takers; he didn't hire them himself. So the projector-man, Mr. Halbert, a big John Henry–looking man, took one look at me and said, "She'll do." I thought there'd be more to getting work than that. He didn't even ask me what my grades were in high school. He just said, "She'll do."

The projector-man is a tall, brown-skinned man, the color of candied yams, and looks like John Henry, like I said, or my imagination of that steel-driving man. He's no Sidney Poitier or the handsome fellows of your generation, though. And he don't ask for references or anything. Like I said, he don't ask how many grades I've been to. He knows Alberta and Turk, and he's looking at her like she's somebody he's fond of and he just looks at me and says matter-of-factly, "She'll do."

"She's an honest young lady and a hard worker," says my sister.

But he ignores her comment and does ask me to say "Ticket, please."

I repeat it. "Ticket, please."

No, what I really say is, "T-t-t-ticket, please?"

"Does she stutter?" he asks Alberta.

"Naw, she doesn't stutter," says Alberta. "She's just nervous."

"Say it again," says the projector-man.

I say, "Ticket, pelase." This time I don't stutter. I just mispronounce the "please."

He doesn't comment. He just gives me another matter-of-fact look and then he says, "She'll do."

Then he says, "She'll look mighty pretty taking them tickets."

My sister Alberta says, "You don't hire a gal for pretty." She mutters something to herself that I don't hear.

The projector-man hires me anyway.

Before I went to get the job as the ticket taker, Alberta took me to this beauty parlor that's also on Race Street, because she told me it made me look too country with my hair not straightened, and I was in the city now, in one of the central cities, and a grown woman. Alberta was sitting reading *Liberty Magazine* while the woman doing my hair started talking about our country going to war.

"Us ain't going to war," said Alberta.

"Us going to war," said the hairdresser.

The hairdresser says she knows a woman who used to be a jazz singer in Berlin until Hitler sent all the jigaboo entertainers outta Germany. I hadn't heard the word "jigaboo" before and didn't know anyone from our part of the world who'd been to Germany. But that hairdresser woman called every type of colored person jigaboo.

Colored Americans, Africans, Caribbeans, Asians and Indians and such. Everybody was a jigaboo who wasn't white. And even some of the whites she referred to as jigaboos.

At first she said that woman told her it was just a rumor that Hitler was going to send all the jigaboo entertainers out of Berlin. First he banned playing jazz on the radio and then the word came down that all the jigaboo entertainers were banished from Germany.

"She's in Switzerland now," said the hairdresser.

"How did y'all meet?" asked Alberta.

"She was passing through our town. Had an entertainment engagement at the Lyric and was looking for someone to do her hair and they sent for me. She said I did a fine job and sometimes we correspond. She wanted me to travel with her and do her hair on the road.

"But that's not the type of person I am. I've got my own shop and I prefer to be my own person."

As for me, I'd just come from a little country town near Covington, Kentucky, and here she was talking about Switzerland and such like places and how she turned down the opportunity to travel about the world with a famous entertainer.

Then she showed us a picture of this woman, her entertainer friend. I'm expecting some high-fancy type. A glamorous type beside a Duesenberg or one of those Mercedes-Benzes like you see in the picture books and magazines, but she shows us a little brown-skinned, sweet-faced woman standing beside a bicycle. And she's wearing knickers. Knickerbockers, I think they call them.

And she shows another picture of the woman standing beside a tall African, a Guyanese but born in London, she tells us. His eyes look like stars in his dark face. And then there's another picture of them walking along a riverbank and there are birds in the sky behind them. I think they are lovers, but the hairdresser says those are publicity photos, and he's some kind of jazz instrumentalist who accompanies her entertainer friend when she sings.

And they both had to settle in another country, but neither wanted to return to the States.

"She still thinks I made a mistake staying in this country when I had the opportunity to see the world."

She greases my hair with a hairdressing with a nice fragrance like coconuts, and she's still talking about us going to war.

"We can't stay ostriches," she says.

After the beauty parlor is when Alberta takes me to town and buys me some jigsaw sandals and a new beige and yellow suit with padded shoulders, the kind in style in those days, the kind that Paulette Goddard used to wear. No, not a zoot suit. It was the men who wore the zoot suits and that was in forty-something, the Black and Latin men. You've heard about those zoot-suit wars?

When I came back from ticket taking, I could hear them, the couple in the duplex next door. Then I hear footsteps out the back door. No, it's not Turk and Alberta; I know it's the couple next door.

I had started to stay in that little country town, but it's Alberta who sent for me. I didn't come to the city just on my own. She started telling me about the new colored theater and that there might be a job for me there. She told me there wasn't anything for me in that little country town but to work in some white folks' kitchen. I told her that there were plenty of white folks' kitchens in Lexington to work in. But she told me they were hiring at a new Black theater in town, a new colored theater.

Alberta and Turk both have factory jobs, working in a tobacco factory. They both work on the line. I don't know what working on the line means. But Alberta says they both work on the line. And they have also worked in the fields, stripping tobacco. But they prefer to work on the line. She didn't want me to work there, though, because she says I'm a more delicate person.

Now I'm sitting here waiting while Alberta is having her hair done. I'm reading *Liberty Magazine*, reading about Andy Hardy and Freddie Bartholomew and the adventures of the Notorious Sophie Lang.

"Us going to war," says the hairdresser.

"No us ain't," insists my sister Alberta.

SHUGER'S WIFE

1.

I've darkened in the Caribbean sun and now I'm the color of polished mahogany and like in Walter Roberts's poem "I ride the white sea horses onto the beach," and it's good to charge from the ocean, into the leaning palms, and to laugh into the sun.

My husband's brought me here to the Caribbean, to an island that the tourists haven't discovered yet, and so I won't give you its name. Even in postcards, I don't name it, and the postcards are always posted from the mainland.

Those who have known me on other islands might say that here I've begun to glow.

We've rented a small house that's separated from the sea by a forest. It's curious that my husband's chosen such a house, but he insists that it's the only rentable house, and anyway, he says, it's not separated from the sea by a true forest but only an accumulation of trees. If you knew him, you wouldn't be surprised by his vocabulary. Mine is more simple and straightforward. I know a forest when I see one. And I know the forest from the trees.

I've come to the seaside. I, like all the others, cannot deny the sea. Another poet said so. Perhaps it was Lamming who said you remember it, always. Anyway, a true poet said so. It must have been Lamming. Even a stranger here, even those from lands without seashores, or even rivers, are drawn to the sea. If I were a poet, I'd hunt for metaphors, or symbolism, but the sea seems to be its own metaphor, its own symbolism.

I take a book with me, one that my husband presented me with: Don Steele's *Symbolism and Modernity*. It is written in the sort of language my husband uses. There is an essay on Hesse's "Der Dichter." I must get my husband to translate the German. He says the author has written other books, not just aesthetics.

There is one on the economic philosophy of Malcolm X and another . . . "I must get you the other books . . . The true meaning . . ." he starts to say, then he quotes from one of the essays:

> The symbolists believed like ancient magicians that words possessed a power to control nature. Each natural force had a secret word to which it was enslaved, and the possessor of the word could control that force, like "abracadabra." Theoretically, one could by mere words control the planets and stars. Poetry was viewed at the apex of words. The poet was the seer, the high priest, capable with his musical chants of bringing down the mountains. Whether any poet, priest or magician has ever accomplished anything resembling such a structure of words to perform miraculous feats is for us here moot.
>
> What is indisputable, however, is that words do have a powerful effect on human emotions and in history. Words can produce sublimity, laughter, cheers, smiles and love. Or, words can produce pain, fear, hatred, melancholy and death. Words can transcend time and picture life thousands of years ago. Words can transform space and picture life on the other side of earth from where one stands.

A sea turtle, on the white sand, near my feet, is in its shell, dreaming.

I daydream.

2.

One can be as corrupted by islands as anything. "If I'm set on getting islands, others are set on worse," says Sancho. My favorite author used to be Cervantes, and I wasn't content to read him in translation. I insisted on learning the original, uncorrupted Spanish.

As for me, perhaps it's only the paradises that corrupt, or what we presume to be the paradises. I'm not set on getting islands, really. If you're born on islands like these, they say, you see the island differently, you view it differently. Islanders, they say, want to escape the island to the mainland. Is the mainland, then, their paradise? If I were born here, perhaps the sea would not amaze and entice me. I wouldn't paint it or try to get its true tones. I wouldn't gather scavenger objects from the beaches to form into sculptures.

3.

In the evening, Sugar and I—sometimes I call him Sugar, not Shuger—are getting dressed to meet friends at a local pub. They call them pubs here. One friend's a movie extra and the other's a poet. Not a poet I've read. But my husband seems to know all the writers I've never read. He doesn't know them all personally. He collects their books. In the bar—I prefer to call it a bar—I drink warm beer. The movie extra, who's never had a speaking part and insists she doesn't want one, insists she prefers being an extra, is silent. But the poet is very talkative. He asks me, "How does one state the whole truth and remain poetic?" At first I think he's speaking to my husband, because it's a question for my husband, not for me.

I don't answer. I pretend I'm a movie extra. I sip the warm beer and watch a few early lovers dance. I hum to the music, but I'm somewhere behind the beat.

Perhaps it's a rhetorical question. Perhaps I'm not expected to answer.

"Were you born on this island?" I ask him finally.

"No, not this one. But another one. One quite like it. One very much the same."

"I've been to Cat Island," I say.

"Yes, Shuger told me you trekked there."

And then he quotes me from one of his own poems.

Something between the empire and home, in an unpoetical time. I suppose to everyone, their age and time seem unpoetical. The more you learn of history. The more you know.

I listen, but I'm unsure of the rhythms of this place. I'm either behind the beat or ahead of it. I can tell that he's as preoccupied with metaphors as my husband, Shuger (that's his last name; he says it was originally spelled Shuyger, but an ancestor changed the spelling; I don't know if that's true ancestral history). Anyway, Shuger pours more beer for me from an orange pitcher, holding the pitcher by only one of its ears.

"Anyway, here's the book I told you about," says my husband, and hands him a copy of Kambon Obayani's *Island of Song*.

My husband likes to present books as gifts. That's his favorite type of gifting. His first gift to me was a book. An autographed copy of a book by Gwendolyn Brooks.

I want to ask this poet whether he too has seen the white sea horses, but I don't. The moon peeks through the window at us. We stay in the pub till the birds wake up and the sun rises out of a cavern of stars.

4.

Walking back on the beach in the sand, I ask whether the hoofprints I see are the hoofprints of mules.

"They're the hoofprints of memory," says the poet.

Then he chants:

Listen to the grass, the ping-pong drums,
The wul'

The movie extra is silent and Shuger is holding me by the waist.

"Wul'?" I whisper.

"World," he says. "That's how my people pronounce 'world.'"

I say nothing. I think of Margaret Walker Alexander's *For My People*. I see a sea turtle and wonder if it's the same one I saw early in the day. Now it's not sleeping but rushing seaward, as turtles rush, scrambling the sand.

Shuger and I enter what I insist is a forest, while the others continue up the beach.

Although Shug is scientifically minded, he collects the poetry of Black men, their writings in general really, from all across the diaspora; some I've heard of, some names I don't know. Fiction, poetry, memoir, essays, all types, you name it. He says that as a Black boy growing up in Minnesota, he felt like an "endangered species"; then his father gave him a copy of Richard Wright's *Black Boy*, the first book he fell in love with, and as he grew older he kept discovering others, from the old school to the new school. He has almost everybody in his collection, names I know and don't know. James Alan McPherson, Ishmael Reed, Michael S. Harper, Clarence Major, Kambon Obayani, John Wideman, Robert Fleming, Jupiter Hammon, James Baldwin, Ralph Ellison, Chester Himes, Sterling Brown, Ernest Gaines, Amos Tutuola, Amiri Baraka, Walter Mosley, Claude McKay, Henry Dumas, Samuel R. Delany, Martin Delany, Olaudah Equiano, Ronald Fair, Rudolph Fisher, Leon Forrest, Sam Greenlee, John A. Williams, George Moses Horton, George Schuyler, Albert Murray, Don

Steele, J. A. Rogers, Robert Hayden, Haki Madhubuti, Dudley Randall, Eric Walrond, Henry Van Dyke, Malcolm X . . . among many others . . .

He even has unpublished manuscripts by every type of Black man, including some incarcerated men, who found out by some means of his collection of books by Black men and sent him copies of their books and manuscripts, fiction, memoirs, poetry, and plays.

In fact, his collection of books and broadsides and manuscripts by Black men authors takes up our whole library at our home in Detroit and even the hallways. I keep my women authors' books in the attic, which I have turned into a library. Once my husband came up to the attic and thought he would be entering a space "for colored girls only," and then discovered that I had books by women of every color, race, creed, and nationality. He started fingering some of the books. I peeked up from my peacock chair and my own reading to glimpse who he was looking at: Carlene Hatcher Polite, Marguerite Duras, Ruby Zagoren, Margaret Randall, Joan Didion, Isabel Allende, Ann duCille, and a few others.

"What's this one about?" he asked.

"It's about a modern-day Black female picara—she's from the lower classes but moves about among people of different levels of society and different races and nationalities. She also sort of got the idea from James Joyce's HCE."

"Say what?"

"You know, 'Here Comes Everybody.' Joyce's expression in one of his books. She was a fan of James Joyce, and even took a course on Joyce when she was in college from the widow of Randall Jarrell, the famous poet."

"Say who?"

"Randall Jarrell. Well, anyway the woman, the lead character, in the book's a bit of a rogue, you know, like the old picaros and picaras of the Spanish tradition."

"Who's Kelly Brown?" he asks, picking up another book.

"That's the title of the book, not the author."

"The woman on the cover is blue."

"She's supposed to be biracial, a woman born of an interracial affair in Kentucky in the old days when interracial relationships were against the law, you know, and then she likewise marries outside of her race. The book's about her adventures and misadventures . . ."

"So it says," he says, looking at the blurb on the back. "And who's Ruby Zogaren?"

"Zagoren. Her book is called *Venture for Freedom*; it's a slave-narrative novel, but she's a Jewish woman."

I know he noticed the book because there's a Black man on the cover. The subtitle is "The True Story of an African Yankee."

He opens the book and starts reading sections aloud:

"'When first plunging into the research necessary for writing *Venture for Freedom*, I did not realize how many individuals would help in the unremitting search for historical facts. My husband . . .'" Then he plunges into the book: "'In the forest of Guinea in West Africa, near a small village, a boy was tracking lion spore . . .'"

"Venture Smith was a real person," I comment.

"I know. That's what it says here. She's got a different last name from her husband."

"I know. I met her daughter when I was visiting a friend at Connecticut College. She's the one who gave me a copy of the book; I mean the friend. We were all sitting at the Black table, you know how we did in those days, and this white girl came up and sat down, and people didn't seem to notice her presence except for me. There was another white-looking girl at the table who turned out to be Black, so I wasn't sure what this one's identity was either. Both had Jewish last names. And then my friend introduced her, and when we got back to her dorm room she gave me a copy of Ms. Zagoren's book and also a copy of a poem by her daughter that had been published in *The Nation* when she was still a schoolgirl."

He puts the book down and picks up another, by a Latina.

"I met her at Connecticut College also. She's from the Dominican Republic. She was still a young girl. She and my friend were both students of June Jordan, you know, the Black woman poet, who was filling in for a poet named William Meredith when he was on sabbatical, I think. You know, they were just beginning to hire Black professors. Some of those colored girls had never had Black professors before. Unlike myself. Anyway, I met a lot of writers when I was a student, writers and future writers of every type and description. I met more writers than I did artists. You introduced me to Dudley Randall, who founded Broadside Press. You remember."

"Of course. You adore writers more than artists anyway. You don't have to compete with them."

"You were telling him about that prisoner who had sent you some of his writings. And then you were thinking of following Mr. Randall's lead and setting up your own publishing company to publish all those manuscripts you were collecting. You wanted his advice. He seemed like a good sort. I mean, Mr. Randall. I liked him."

"And who's Zona Gale?"

I tell him.

"Who's Carlene Hatcher Polite?"

"That's Toni Morrison's cousin, someone told me. I was sitting on this wall at grad school outside the dorm reading Toni Morrison, and someone walked by and tossed up to me a copy of a book by Carlene Hatcher Polite, and said she was Toni Morrison's cousin. I didn't know if she was signifying or meaning her real honest-to-goodness cousin. It's a very experimental type book. I read them both. I think even you'd like Carlene Hatcher Polite."

"I like her name." He thumbs through the other book. "This picara sounds a bit like you."

I say nothing.

"'Here Comes Everybody' is right. They should call you HCE. And you're a bit of a rogue yourself. You've got every imaginable female up here. It's a bit crowded, don't you think? I notice you don't have any artwork by women artists, not even your own."

Then he stands among Native American female authors and fingers my dream catcher.

"So this is your dream catcher."

Then he's among the Latinas again. Then he lifts up a book by Mary Barber and stands among the Irish female writers.

"I guess I never really thought about Irish women writers. I didn't know there were so many Irish female writers. I know all the men of course. I think I read Mary McCarthy, but she's Irish American, isn't she?"

He goes among the "colored girls" again and picks up Alice Walker's *In Love and Trouble.*

"That's the first Alice Walker book I ever read," I said. "She came to our school and gave a reading. She was supposed to give a lecture but forgot her notes, and so gave a reading instead. She read from that book. My professor introduced us. She thought I was a writer, a poet maybe. Alice Walker, I mean. But I told her I was an art student. But I was taking courses in African American literature from this professor, and some of us students were introduced to her."

He muses a moment, replaces *In Love and Trouble*, then gives me some papers to sign, why he came up to the attic in the first place. Some sort of new homeowner's insurance policy form that we both had to sign.

Then he's drawn to another book with a Black man on the cover.

"Who's this?"

"He's supposed to be a private detective, part African American and part Russian. A sort of satire on the detective genre. There are a series of stories. That's the same author who wrote *Kelly Brown*. And that's some science fiction. I guess they call it Afrofuturism now. That section is all her books. When she wrote that it was the 1950s, though. Her real first name is Electra, but they used to tease her when she was a child and call her Electricity. So she started using her second name as her first name. Her father's Hawaiian. Spanish and Hawaiian. Her mother's African American and Irish. That's a childhood memoir over there and there's a family history.

"Her grandfather founded one of those little freetowns.

"That one was called Warthumtown. It wasn't just an all-Black town, though. They had some white people and some Mexicans and some Native American families too. But it was owned by Blacks, a free Black founded the town."

"You've got a whole section."

"Yah. Those are the indie authors over there. I've got whole sections on them. And I've got my own collection of manuscripts too."

"It's really tight up here. You're really crowded."

"It's my cocoon."

"What about the movie extra? Has she never had a speaking part?" I'm asking now. "When you called her your friend, I thought it was going to be a man. Are she and the poet lovers?"

"No, they had just met that night."

"They could still be lovers."

"No, she's never had a speaking role. But there's not a movie set in the Caribbean that I haven't seen her in. She loves playing extras in Caribbean scenes, and they love to have her. I think she was even in a James Bond movie as a little girl, somewhere in the background."

I try to remember what movies set in the Caribbean that I've seen her in. I try to remember James Bond. I try to remember a little girl or a grown woman. Carrying a tray of seafood? Dancing on a table or the beach? Lounging in the sand? Riding the white sea horses up from the sea? She has one of those familiar faces. An everywoman's face.

"And the poet? Tell me one of his poems."

Shuger recites:

Change confirms the truth of change
In an exotic setting
Where love is many colored

And then he recites more poems. He has one of those sorts of memories, both auditory and photographic. Poems of moons, stars, boats, sea turtles, the sea itself, caverns, awakened birds, more stars, silence, ecstasy and dreams, and here and there are cocoa beans, mango, and bamboo.

5.

Inside the forest house, Shuger and I make love.

From the open window, the moon's so bright. I nest against him like a sea turtle and wonder if the ocean ever sleeps. In a dream, I play a movie extra, but it's an old silent movie.

When I'm half awake, the sun strides through the window shouting up up up get up! I shower in a wooden shower stall, but I'd expected a cruder, older one. Nothing so modern. I can smell the lavender from the shaving soap.

"Are they lovers?" I insist.

"No, they're married."

"So you lied when you said they'd just met."

"It's a private joke."

"That's no joking matter."

"He says whenever he's with her, it's always like he's meeting her for the first time. She almost never speaks. I've almost never heard a peep from her. It's like she's a movie extra in her own life too."

"Have they been married for a long time?"

"Rather long."

"Maybe they know each other too well. Do they have kids?"

"Several."

"Aha!"

I wash my hair. I imagine their children as little movie extras, running about or riding seahorses. But he says their kids are grown-ups now. Grown children. Not little ones.

6.

From the window, I see Shuger, dressed and walking through the forest toward the beach. He's carrying one of his books. *Island of Song*? *Symbolism and Modernity*? *Images of Kin*? The odor of aftershave mixed with peppermint toothpaste lingers. I arrive on the beach with buttered rolls and melons.

After breakfast, the two of us walk the shoreline. Out to sea are fishermen in tiny bamboo-colored boats. Some drag in nets; others hold poles or harpoons. Real harpoons. Not Raymond Barrow's harpoons of light. I've never seen real harpoons before, not even from a distance.

There used to be pirates all along these coasts, says Shuger. I mishear him.

It sounds like he said, "There used to be pirates all along these coats." Then I hear him right.

"Oh, yeah? Suppose there are now? I saw this news story about modern-day pirates. Drug smugglers."

"I suppose," he says, matter-of-factly. "But this isn't the Bahamas."

I picture Shuger and me as two pirates. Not modern-day pirates, but pirates of the old days.

Buccaneers. The fishermen look so small in the ocean. But we, Shuger and I, must look equally small to them. Or perhaps smaller.

He sits on the sand, opens a book, and begins to read.

7.

At the edge of the beach, a woman is breaking stones. The dress she wears is cactus green; sunlight dances on her hammer.

"Why is she breaking stones?" I ask Shuger.

Shug doesn't answer right away, as if he's pondering the question, or thinks I'm ignorant for asking.

"All she does all day is break stones," he says finally. "It earns her a living."

He returns to reading.

I picture her from sunset to sunrise, breaking stones. I picture a whole island of stone breakers. Men, women, children. They get up early to go break stones.

The wind ruffles my hair. I hand him a melon. We eat juicy melons. I watch the woman break stones. I'm so thirsty I could swallow the whole ocean.

"Maybe she won't sell them," I muse. "Maybe she'll just use them to build her own cottage."

"She'll sell them," he says. "The masons buy from her."

That's how they
Turn stones into bread

8.

I sit on the sand and listen to the rhythm of the stone breaker. I don't dare speak to her. Although we're the same color, she knows I'm not of this island. I tell myself I don't speak because I don't want to break the rhythm of her stone breaking. Shug has returned to the forest house, but I stay to listen to the woman breaking stones and to watch the seahorses rise higher and the men in their boats rise with them. I watch the sea turtle. Is it still the same one?

Shug has told me about them, the sea turtles. They come to lay their eggs in the sand. They lay their eggs in a shallow layer of sand, and so the eggs are ripe for predators.

"Why don't they lay them in deeper sand?" I asked.

"Because the eggs are too fragile for deeper sand," he answered.

And when the tiny turtles are born, they make their way toward the sea. If the seabirds don't get them. If the seabirds don't get them, they return to the sea.

"Would you rather be a seabird or a tortoise?" I asked.

"It's not a tortoise; it's a turtle," he replied. "They're not the same."

"What's the difference?" I asked.

"The tortoise is strictly a land dweller."

"And the other one, does the other one dwell strictly at sea?"

He didn't reply. Then he said the word "terrapin." Then he talks of tortoises, the giant ones of the Galapagos Islands.

Now I watch the sea turtle scoop out a nest of sand. And then it covers its nest with the thinnest layer of sand. Then it turns seaward. When it reaches the sea, it climbs a white seahorse and rides further out.

I, on shore, watch a seabird land near the turtle's nest. It takes flight as I rise. One fisherman moves inland from the sea, and I climb through sand.

I lift a seashell that has found its way into the forest.

I think of Lamming's sea and then Collymore's.

Caribbean poets form a book that Shuger gave me before we came to this island.

9.

I'm on the beach again, watching the woman break stones. I light a cigarette.

"Give me one," she says.

I rise and give her the whole package.

"Not the whole package, my dear. Just one," she says, as if she's scolding me. She takes one cigarette and returns the package.

"Are you drawing me?" she asks. I show her my sketchbook.

"That's me all right," she says. "You must be very clever to draw so fast. A lot of artists come here. On holiday. But they don't draw so fast. They take their time."

I think she's going to say something else, but she doesn't. She goes on breaking stones.

I close my sketchbook as she poses her hammer over a stone.

"You Shuger's wife, aren't you?" she asks.

I wonder how she knows him and not me. I nod and wait for her to explain how she knows him, but she doesn't. She goes on breaking stones.

10.

I move forward, toward the edge of the sea, trying not to disturb the shallow turtles' nests.

I toss the butt end of my cigarette into the ocean and watch it float in a nest of seaweed. I think it's against the law to toss cigarettes into the sea, but I do so anyway.

Roguish me.

11.

In the pub I sip warm beer.

I ask my husband how the stone breaker knows his name.

"Because I told her. She asked me and I told her."

"Were you chatting her up?"

He ignores me.

"She thought I was a native of the islands. She knew you weren't. But she thought I was."

I finish the beer, and we go swimming in the starlight. We ride the white sea horses. We charge from the ocean into the leaning palms.

Back in the rented house, I dream of a woman somewhere breaking stones.

"I didn't know that people still said 'native,'" I whisper. "Not in this modern day and age."

THE FEMALE ANGEL

The female angel walked across the Seine

—ROMARE BEARDEN

I am the angel that Romare Bearden—or, I should say, I am the female angel that Romare Bearden once claimed he saw in Paris. It must've been around 1950, although this is a purely human conception of time and space. It might have been the Middle Ages in Spain or India, or the time of the Pharaohs in Egypt. It might have been when Kush was an African empire, or the time of the Ethiopian kings. It might have been the time of the Neanderthals or the Cro-Magnons. Perhaps I stood next to a cave artist in Europe, or with Huang-ti of China. Perhaps I was there at the time of Hammurabi's laws. I have known Chinese scholars and Jewish prophets. Was I not there when the Buddha was born, or Confucius? Did Meng-tse the philosopher know me? And what of Asoka of India or Hannibal the Great? Did Cicero know me, or Augustine? What of Attila and Muhammad? Genghis Khan? Kublai Khan? Was I not there when Ignatius of Loyola founded the Society of Jesus? And what of Jesus Himself? Did not Toussaint Louverture know me when he led his revolt, and what of Simón Bolívar? And Jose de San Martin? Did not Gandhi know me? And Jawaharlal Nehru? Did Malcolm ever know me? Or Mandela? Or perhaps I am only the female angel that Romare Bearden, artist, claimed he saw in Paris. I have walked across the Seine, according to Romare.

And sometimes he would tell his friends the story about me, especially his fellow artist friends, who delight in metaphor and symbolism.

But always Romare, it is believed, thought I was a product of his imagination, because someone—was it one of his Turkish friends?—had given him the wrong brand of cigarette, so the story goes. Or perhaps it's my own imagination. Perhaps it was the right brand of cigarettes but not the brand of cigarettes he thought it was or requested. In those days, people smoked a lot of cigarettes, you know, even in the movies. He thought they were Gauloises that the someone, perhaps a Turk, had given him. But they turned out, it seems, to have contained hashish. Being an angel, I shouldn't tell this lie, if it is a lie. If it was not the Turk who'd given him the cigarettes, not the French brand Gauloise, then it was from someone from North Africa, Morocco maybe, one of my ancestors.

If from Morocco, then it was from one of the cities, maybe Casablanca, Rabat, Fes, Erfoud, Marrakech or Essaouira, Volubilis, Mehenes. I'm not sure all of those are even true names, but I would prefer the Moroccan story. If indeed it was Moroccan, to be from Casablanca or Marrakech, for these are places mostly familiar to me, or my ancestor, and I have often been an angel in Casablanca or in Marrakech, though often in Marrakech I'm never mistaken for an angel. Do you mistake me for an angel?

In Casablanca, at the mosque of King Hassan II, I am an angel among the thousands of worshippers. I know most everyone in Casablanca, from the beggars to the diplomats. I know Paris and London as well as Medina. I have been an angel dining in the Restaurant L'Entrecote. Sometimes I'm a dark angel, sometimes as blonde as anyone in the picture books.

Sometimes some have beckoned me like they were the sultans and the whole world their pleasure dome. I am an angel among the mimosa trees of Fes. I am an angel among the cork trees of Fes, engaged in my own botanical studies.

I am an angel eating wheat bread with butter and drinking mint tea from a tall glass trimmed with arabesque designs. The man sitting at a table across from me looks like a Grand Vizier. Tell me again of your medieval cities, for I have roamed them like any good angel. I know all the theological colleges. Let me read my holy books amidst the spice markets. My hair is the color of henna.

Did any of you see me too?

In Morocco, in the land of my ancestors, I now know all the medinas, all the old cities. I know all the holy cities and the holiest city. Shall I combine in me the African, the Berber, and the Arab? I bathe in a Moorish bath. I know the art of the mosaic. I drink a cocktail in a palm grove. I overhear a man tell a woman he loves or thinks he loves, "You are the treasure of Morocco, you are the treasure of Marrakech, you are the treasure of Fes."

I dance among the argana trees. I dance among the olive trees. I am in a white and blue villa. I stand among the merchants of Marrakech. I charm the fishermen. I am in a café in the medina. My wrists are full of golden jewelry. I am a sculptress. I stand among the thuya trees. Do you call me an angel only in Paris?

Anyway, at some point in the story, I appeared, a female angel, crossing the Seine.

Have any of you seen me too?

HORSE RACE

A fragment

I'm visiting my friends. He's Mexican and she's African American. They're husband and wife, but you can't tell if she's Mexican or he's African American.

They're the same complexion. They take me to a horse race. I sit silently watching the races, while they talk to each other. Sometimes they talk in Spanish, sometimes English. Sometimes a combination of both.

They're both farmworkers. She midwives the mares on a horse farm while he takes care of the ponies, the *caballitos*. His name is Federico and hers is Martha.

Sometimes he calls her Marta or Martita. She prefers Marta.

Oh, what a horse! Ay, que caballo. I bet on that one. I don't bet on the horses, myself; I bet on the jockeys, says Martha.

But it's the horses that win. That one's very good. Ese es muy bueno. I helped raise that horse, so I know he's good.

And I midwifed the mare that bore him. A good jockey makes a better horse. I'll stand by what I'm saying. I'll bet on the jockeys every time.

While I'm listening to them I'm thinking of the story that Martha told me about how they first met. She didn't know he was Mexican until he opened his mouth to speak, and he didn't know she was American until she opened her mouth to speak. They were working on the same farm before they started speaking to each other. And the first question she asked him was whether he was married or single. She thought he might be working to send money home to his wife and children in Mexico. But she claims she thought he was one of us till he started speaking, coaxing one of the little horses. *Caballito*. And he thought she was *la raza* till she started speaking to one of the mares, "Yes, my girl."

He's a little bit shorter than she is, and she's a little bit older than him. But Martha says when one falls in love it's like magic. Now they're speaking Spanish and I don't understand a word of it. Except when she says the sun is very hot out here, and then she asks him if he still has enough money, if he didn't bet it all on that horse. I can tell that type of talk in anybody's language.

She tells me about how all over the farms, there's a great demand for her midwifery. And she brags about her husband and says he raises the best little horses, the best *caballitos*, in all Kentucky.

She talks about how he came courting her first, before he asked her to marry him. How he preferred to court a woman first. She made some sweet potato pie for him.

Then he told her the story of Africana. It seems that the slave ship she was riding in neared Mexico. They took the slaves on deck to exercise them, and she jumped in the water and made for the shore. They were too far from the coast for her to swim, they were sure, and besides who could swim in chains? But it's said, she made the shore anyway, like magic, like a miracle. People in the little village called her *la esclava*, and everyone agreed she could cure almost anything.

I always bet on the jockeys, she's repeating.

And for me it's the *caballitos*. I raised them, so I know them.

As for me, they think I'm a bit of a rogue, because I bet on neither horse nor rider.

BATHTUB GIN

A fragment

I'm making me some bathtub beer, like in the old days when they usedta make bathtub gin. Except bathtub beer is legal now, artisan beers, and they've got a lot of bathtub beer clubs even. My girlfriend Migi, who grew up sometimes on the reservation and sometimes in the big city, is sitting in the living room watching TV. I've got me one of those big-screen televisions that's programmable.

Migi's almost forty and I'm over forty. She calls herself a social historian and even went to college to study the subject. Because of the nature of her dissertation, she had to watch TV a lot and every now and then returns to the reservation and every now and then returns to the big city.

She has a friend who reminds me of Oprah but who wears her hair like Whoopi Goldberg. I'm not sure that's why she chose her for a friend.

Sometimes the three of us sit around drinking bottles of my bathtub beer and watch TV.

I design artisan beer for the company and bathtub beer for myself and my friends.

Migi likes for me to talk about Harlem in the 1920s when all the decadent, prosperous people used to come slumming, and I'm not even from Harlem. I'm from Kentucky. She also likes to read about Berlin in the 1930s and that whole history.

And of course she reads about the history of her own people and returns again and again to the reservation but won't stay there.

Her friend tells her about the colored showgirls in Berlin who weren't considered very good in New York but played the nightclubs in Berlin and wrote some story about them feasting on lobster Newburg and drinking first-class champagne until Hitler chased them all out of Germany. She likes to research the history of non-Aryans in Germany. They met, I think, in some social history museum. She's one of those indie-type writers who publishes her own works and supports independent and local bookstores. I think she even owns her own bookstore. She reminds me of those old-time "race women" and "race men" that they used to have in the old days. She banks with a Black-owned bank and invests in Black-owned businesses. Migi is doing the same on the reservation, except with the Native Americans. Sometimes they pool their money together and invest in these businesses.

I think she's part Narragansett, a native of Washington State, but the reservation she goes to is in Arizona. There are thousands of tribes, but I can only name so many.

We're watching reruns of *Columbo*, who always catches the one who dunnit.

I think Columbo's smart, but Migi thinks it's pure intuition. She says he's an intuitionist. I say it has everything to do with smarts.

Sometimes the women talk jazz and about the rebels who would listen to jazz all over Europe, how the subversives would listen to jazz. And Migi talks about some sort of music that's only allowed to be heard by Native Americans themselves and only on the reservation, not like that jazz traveling all around the world.

Her friend is showing her old photographs of female jazz singers from the 1920s and 1930s. One of them is dressed in nankeen trousers; I think that's what they're called.

Bodacious, those women, I hear her say. I call them wrens, because they say those are the birds with the sweetest song.

Migi is also documenting native medicines, or rather natural medicines, and once made me a tonic of powdered mustard seeds. You could even eat it and put it on your fish cakes.

"Here you go, girl; try this," I say.

"He was a math whiz in college," says Migi. "He's the one who taught me. They got a tutor for me and sent him. I was surprised when he turned up a Black man; they were talking about this math genius, you know, and he was just as surprised to see me.

"Sometimes we'd study in my dorm room, where I had dream catchers. Sometimes we'd study in his dorm room, where he had this poem by Benjamin Banneker pinned to his wall.

"'A Mathematical Problem in Verse,' it was called. I didn't even know that Benjamin Banneker wrote poetry. What is it you taught me, darling?"

I don't answer.

"We became lovebirds," I hear her say.

"Both girls think I'm not living up to my potential.

"Spending my time designing bathtub gin."

"Beer," I correct them.

THE HISTORIAN, THE ACTRESS, AND THE PLAYWRIGHT

The Indians burn pepper and salt as an exorcism whenever the priests come near. They link the new diseases with the Jesuits," the man said with a laugh.

The man who had spoken was a Brazilian playwright. The woman sitting in the middle was a French actress, and the other Brazilian was a historian.

"Why don't you write a play for me around that?" the French actress asked.

"Because, my dear, this young playwright is concerned with a new theater, an international and universal theater, without events."

"How can you write a play without events?" she asked, looking at the man.

"It is not events he wants to deal with," the historian said. "Because events are too colored by one's place and history—one's time, one's prejudices, one's politics. He wants to write a play about the mind and the imagination, an ideal of the spirit; 'A Realm of the Spirit,' I think it will be called, no moments whatsoever."

"But how can it be done and still be a play?" the actress asked. The playwright was silent.

"Ideas in simultaneous time," the historian said. "I don't know what it means. I'm bound by time and memory, by actions. Do you remember when we met, Jeanne?"

"Yes," the woman said.

"Weren't there plots, characters, principal situations, various locales?"

"Yes," she said.

"A range of subjects and ideas and values but only the handmaiden of experience. I'm a lover of action, direct and retrospective."

"I can't imagine a play without any experiences."

"No, that's not what I mean," the young man said.

"Then explain what you mean," the French actress said, displaying a feeling of tenderness for the young man.

The young man was silent.

"Didn't you say something about the play's being about man's relationship to the universe and not to other men?" asked the historian. "Or women," he said, squeezing the woman's arm.

"Are you talking about the unity of man's spirit with God's?" the French actress asked. "I know about that. I've heard other authors talk about that. I can understand that. But still there are scenes. I can't do a play without scenes. But then the play can't be written for me. I like intense, emotional moments. I can only be a passionate woman, or sometimes a cold one, but acting against other people's emotions."

She made her eyes flash and then look very icy. She was nursing a cold and took a handkerchief from her bosom and blew her nose. She was a beautiful woman in her late twenties with jet-black hair.

"Maybe I'll explain better," the historian said.

"Why doesn't he speak for himself?" the woman asked.

"Oh, he never speaks," the historian said. "He never says anything. I've met him several times. I remember his works, but I can never remember his name, because he never says anything. Every time I meet him, I forget who he is. Though if someone were to say, 'A Realm of the Spirit,' I would remember the work."

"It's written already?" the woman asked with excitement.

"Oh, the design for it is," the historian said. "Imagine my trying to write history without creating men and women and their lives. And ideas," he added. "But only the conflict of ideas and spirits and values. No moments. No perspectives in time. Never being brought into the presence of anyone. What would that make for? I can't see the universe except through experiences. Didn't you write some play about a woman whose eyes reflected the universe and another one about the universe inside yourself?"

The playwright nodded but explained that he was younger then and more romantic.

"He speaks," the woman said, touching him with affection. "You shouldn't be such a hidden one."

"And another about a man who allows the soul of a god to enter him."

"And about a prophet—a man whose actions predict the future. Not his ideas, but his actions, and things are created or uncreated, and then about a god who makes himself and then the rest of us. Still there were events, encounters, experiences. 'But the experiences were the handmaidens to the ideas. These are plays with all experience and no idea. I want simply to reverse that. All ideas and no experience.' Is that what you mean?" he asked the young playwright.

The playwright continued to look at him.

"Well, we shall see if it can be done. If you can recreate the world of ideas under your pen and only the world of ideas. Let me know when you've completed the task. Do you think he'll succeed?"

The actress said she didn't know but wished him every success in the world.

"I suppose your leading character will have to be one of those eternal and mythical figures who is given a supernatural task and succeeds because a god adopts him. But I suppose it can't even be that. Well, it's not my problem. I can't imagine it. It's outside my imagination. I believe in ordinary men and women, fragments of reality, shards of recollection, the thoughts of a particular man at a particular time. Who knows but that everything we attempt in the world is not . . . Well, I suppose if it's in this world it's a natural task, but who knows what it is in relationship to another world? And dreams, what kind of dreams did men and women have in other times and places? Ah, those kinds of things make me a happy man . . . I thought I saw something out of the corner of my eye. I looked. There was nothing. Do you ever think you see something out of the corner of your eye?"

"All the time," the actress said. Then she said, "I'm drawn to playwrights. They're such fascinating people."

"You're drawn to them because they create your identity for you, my dear. Ah, this woman has many acquaintances out of past characters that have been created. For her, especially, she feels. And she continues to change from one to the other, and various versions of the same person. I never know who she is or who she's going to be, or who she thinks I am. And it delights me. It really does. She's the symbol of the human past for me. My dear, what are you afraid of? But I suppose it's your way of creating possibilities for yourself. Wouldn't that be an interesting play—the nature of this particular woman—her relationship to reality, to the past and present, how she makes use of unreality, fantasies, I think even hallucinations?"

She looked at him. He patted her shoulder.

"How she dislocates time just in her little being. Doesn't that sound delightful?"

The playwright was silent.

"Behold the discursiveness of the uncommunicable," the historian said, raising his hand. "I can read your eyes, sir. Ah, you like the possibilities of that, don't you?"

Again the playwright was silent.

"Do you know he's never written a comedy?" the historian said. "I can just see history as a parade of clowns and self-conscious fools. But this one. Oh, no, he doesn't find any comedy. Oh, this high comedic nation.

"Everything from the beginning. Some of it is sadistic humor but nevertheless. Sir, find some happiness if not meaning in existence. See how he looks at me, puzzled, astonished, the way he looks at the world."

"Do you feel that the present social structure must be destroyed?" the woman asked with compassion.

"He believes in writing, agriculture, and medicine," the historian said with a small laugh.

"Do you believe in humanity and dignity?" the woman asked, leaning closer to him. "All of the great authors believe in that."

"Don't mind her; she's a victim of insanity," the historian said. "She's in the hand of God."

"What?" the playwright asked.

"That is what they call it. Being in the hand of God. She still has the illusion of her divinity, even now." He laughed hard and long.

The playwright looked at the woman and continued to look at her. The historian continued to laugh a very long time.

RAVENNA

Her parents had adopted her because Ravenna was a beautiful child, a joy to look at. She was beige with an oval face and her hair (when it was straightened) was as silky and as black as a raven's wing. She seemed a perfect girl—beautiful, well-behaved.

At the time of the adoption there was another girl.

Both girls were ten. (They wondered how Ravenna got so old before anyone wanted her.) But the other girl was not a beauty. She was Black in the days when Black wasn't considered beautiful. And in all honesty, her face looked like a frog's. Though if she'd been lemon yellow or even beige that feature might have been quietly overlooked.

She was in the same room with Ravenna, hiding against the wing of a table.

The mother was so taken with Ravenna that she hadn't noticed the other child, but the father had noticed her.

"Why don't we adopt her?" asked the father.

"Oh no," she whispered, then drew him into the hall where the girls couldn't hear. "Ravenna's as beautiful as a peacock. I want a child who'd be a joy to look at."

"I meant them both. Why don't we adopt them both?"

"We couldn't afford them both. We'd have to choose."

"Ravenna will get someone to want her, but the other girl . . ."

"How can you be so? I want a child to be a joy."

"Suppose we didn't have this choice?" he asked.

Why was he testing her so; she felt herself as good as anyone, better than most. She was not an evil woman. She was not selfish. But she wanted Ravenna. She wanted a pretty child. If she couldn't have her own.

"I want a child who's a joy."

"We'll ask for them both."

"But, darling, think about it. The little . . ." She started to say "little monster." "The other one will always grow up in the shadow of her sister's beauty. Grow up perverse or jealous. She'll get no smiles."

"We'd treat them both as equals."

"I don't mean us. Of course we'd treat them equally. But strangers. She'll get no smiles from strangers. And when they're together, darling—the other—I didn't ask her name, will shrink against the smiles her sister gets. I want a child who's a joy."

He thought of it for a moment, and though he would have had the heart for them both, he thought of his wife's arguments, and of strangers.

"Okay," he said.

They went back into the playroom where the two girls were. His wife took Ravenna's hands and played with her. He lingered by the table where the other child was hiding. He gave her all the smiles he could. But she wouldn't take the smiles. She rolled her eyes at him, hugged the wing of the table. Still, he lingered near her while the wife and Ravenna played and enjoyed each other.

He wondered at his own motive of affection for the funny-looking child. He himself had been a so-called ugly child, but he had grown up handsome, surprising everyone—even himself.

Perhaps this child wouldn't provide them with as much surprise, but he was drawn to her.

He smiled at her again. She looked at him with dignified indifference. He wondered where she had come by that expression.

"Do you want to go for ice cream?" he asked.

"Are you telling me the truth?" She looked at him suspiciously, her eyes on him, dark, round, protruding.

"I'm telling the truth," he said. "We can go downstairs to the cafeteria and I'll buy you ice cream."

Her eyes lit up. He couldn't imagine them bigger, but they were. He knew she was an intelligent child. He knew she understood.

His wife and Ravenna were sitting in chairs by the window holding hands and laughing.

"What's your name?"

"René."

"Come on, René."

He held his hand out. She took it.

"Where are you going?" his wife asked when they were at the door.

"To get ice cream."

At first she frowned because he hadn't invited them along, and she didn't want to make Ravenna unhappy. "We'll get some later," she told her. Then she smiled at the other girl, but it was a forced smile.

At the cafeteria table, they ate ice cream. The girl kept watching him.

"Are you adopting Ravenna?" she asked.

"I think we're going to."

"Yes, you are. I heard you say you were."

He wanted to promise something. He wanted to make some suggestions. He thought of his wife's forced smile.

"I'll come and visit you," he said. That was the best he could do.

"No you won't."

"Why won't I if I said I would?"

She shrugged, swallowed ice cream. "Because."

"Because?"

She frowned. She struck the table, impatient with his ignorance.

"I'll come as often as I can," he promised.

"Well, if it takes you all that long," she said.

"If it takes me all that long? For what?"

"To look at me good."

THE HORSE-BELIEVING WOMAN

I was new to the neighborhood and the only one to pay special attention, or to take special notice, when this odd species of a woman came galloping by high-spirited; she kicked her heels up, pranced, then trotted past in square-toed, patent-leather boots. As she rounded the corner, I thought I heard her whinnying. There are tales of people who have totems, or spirit animals. Native people tell such tales, and so perhaps her totem or spirit animal was the horse. Either that, or she was just plain crazy. Of course, she could have been both/and or neither one nor the other.

To look at her she seemed quite extraordinary. It was broad daylight, but even if it had been almost dusk, you'd have noticed her and maybe even taken delight, as I did, and there was no mistaking the whinny. No sound but that. And I was certain, too, of the gallop.

Here were two women who came to welcome me to the neighborhood, and these two women went on bantering and seemed to take no special notice of this "horse woman."

"What in the world!" I exclaimed and gave a chuckle. What in the world indeed.

"What in the world, what?" asked Clara.

"That was Grace Moody just rounded the corner," explained Zapora.

I was new to the neighborhood, so I was one to take notice. Perhaps for others she was just ordinary Grace, and no one even remembered to notice.

"Oh, no one pays her any mind," said Clara, as if reading my thoughts and taking new notice of Grace, the wondrous woman.

"How could you not pay her any mind?" I asked. "And what was all that?"

We could hear the whinny again, from a distance. "Oh, she does all that for some reason," said Clara.

"Nobody knows the reason, but she believes herself to be a horse, that's all. At first I thought she just believed in horses when they first told me about this horse-believing woman, but then I learned she believes herself to be an actual horse."

"Did you hear her whinny? I thought I heard a whinny."

"You bet you did," said Zapora. "You bet you did."

They started to banter about something else, as if Grace Moody were no phenomenon at all.

"Well, tell me about Grace Moody," I declared.

"Nothing to tell," said Zapora. "She believes herself to be a horse, is all."

"She must be drunk," I said.

"Never a drop," said Zapora.

"Well, how did she come to believe such a thing?" I asked. I'd started to call it "nonsense," but I didn't really think it was nonsense.

"Nobody knows," replied Zapora. "All the kids in the neighborhood, the little ones, go and ride her and make a game of it. They say she's better than a hobby horse. Her husband . . ."

"You mean, she's married?" I cut in.

"Mr. Jim Moody," said Clara.

"A really lovely man," said Zapora. "The nicest man you'd ever want to know."

"Have to be to put up with that," I said. Again, I didn't say "nonsense."

Zapora gave me a narrow look.

"You all are used to her. I'm not," I explained simply, as Grace Moody rounded the corner again, galloping, prancing.

I thought she would continue up the street, but she paused in front of my porch and stood kicking up her heels, stamping, and whinnying. Yes, indeed, it was a whinny. I just stared at her.

"Grace, this is Amanda, new to the neighborhood." It was Zapora who introduced her. Clara just grinned.

I thought again of totems and spirit animals.

Grace gave me a marvelous and amazed look as if she recognized me but said nothing. She nodded and stood blowing and whinnying. She was a chestnut-brown-skinned woman, and I noticed a white star on her forehead.

I didn't know if it was a birthmark or simply painted on.

It looked like it was painted on, but Zapora and Clara explained later that it was indeed a birthmark, Zapora adding, "Maybe that's why she's horse-believing because she was marked like one."

Nonsense, I wanted to counter, but I didn't.

I noticed that she was wearing thick white socks and a turquoise Indian blanket with a hole cut in the center for her neck like a Mexican poncho, but everyone called it her "horse blanket."

She stood blowing and whinnying and listening to our banter. Rather, Zapora and Clara bantered while I watched Grace, too amazed in her presence to say a word. She too looked amazed, then said, "I'd better fix supper." She said it just like any ordinary woman, then she trotted, or rather pranced, off.

"Married!" I exclaimed. "I can't believe that."

"Believe it," said Zapora.

"She's just a woman with a mysterious imagination," said Clara.

"Extraordinary," said Zapora.

"She looks so wise and knowing, though," I said. "While you were talking, I mean, she was looking so wise and knowing."

"Well, she is wise and knowing," said Zapora.

"Was she like that when he married her?" I asked.

"People say so," said Clara.

"How can a man marry a woman like that?" I asked.

"Men in love don't judge," said Zapora.

"How can a man not judge that?" I declared.

Zapora gave me a narrow look. I didn't say another word.

THE LOST STORIES

Fragments

I. Jazz People

"Come on inside," she says, hugging his waist. "We can get your luggage later. I'm really glad to see you. Daddy will be really glad."

I follow them inside.

We hear the jazz, soft, like a whisper, and tiptoe into the den. He's playing the saxophone with his back to us, facing the corner, the way he used to play on stage, turning his back to the audience, something he'd seen Miles do, and so he started doing the same thing. He understood it. I didn't.

A large man with a broad back, impressive even from the back. Or it's his music. Maybe it's just the music that's impressive. We stand listening, not sure if he's aware we're in the room. His music is a hush, then combat, then a journey into himself, and then he's becoming something beyond himself. It's music that he hides himself in, and then it's almost like a confession.

Unlike Miles he's not a well-known jazz person. He's an obscure jazzman, known only to a few of us devotees.

He turns. He embraces and kisses the young woman whom he calls "Tater" first, then he shakes hands with and hugs his friend Covington, and then he gives me the same aloof look that he sometimes gives his audience. I'm the outsider, the alien, the intruder.

Hey, Jude, the obscure . . .

II. Abstract Fiction

Information about the character is given to you, the reader. Initially, you take the information as authoritative. The story is written in third-person limited omniscient. When you discover the main character is not a madman, you read the story differently. When you thought the character a madman, the description of everything seemed surreal. (Surrealism, a movement in art and literature, refers to the liberation of the unconscious.) There must be some indication of how the character views you, the reader. Is it possible to summarize a viewpoint?

There are many connections between form and character. What each character wants determines character. Sometimes change in character involves irony. At some point in the story, you discover that the viewpoint is unreliable. Perhaps it has been foreshadowed all along.

Is the third-person viewpoint always objective? Describe.

III. Cultural Pluralism

Da hieu. My name Nguyen Smith. I am girl daughter of Mr. Joe Smith and Miss Ko Xuan Truyen. I am half Aframerican, half Vietnamese. Return beginning. Born Saigon 1970. Mr. Joe Smith find me bring me America 1988. Convent school I study be seamstress. I no dumb woman. I no speak the English very well. I speak Vietnamese excellent. I speak French good also. Nun Soeur Clara say I speak French impeccable. I write *quoc-ngu* Vietnamese. I write French. Vietnamese national language. Ban French in North. I from South. I no come America make revolution. I no gorilla. I come here study English. I meet Mr. James Provost. Me . . . Il a fait impression. C'est impossible. Aussi il me porte intérêt. Mr. James Provost begin court me. My father he no like Mr. James Provost, but I like very much. I think he very handsome. I think he very nice man. If he handsome not nice I no like. I no like man just handsome. Must be good man. He ask marry me. I here America. Free say yes. I say yes.

We marry, live Keeneland country. Kentucky. Bluegrass. Mr. James Provost he *homme noir*. I know you thinking him *homme blanc*. He have farm like *homme blanc*. He have many horse. Colt, stallion, filly, foal.

IV. Sweet Marsala

Miss Gilbert used to be a schoolteacher before she went to Hollywood and was in those movies. You know, they always had her playing those real exotic types of island woman. In one of them I seen her prowling about like a cat and making these purring cat noises. Sweet Marsala they used to call her. I seen all those movies she was in. Then after that she started to be in these leading roles—no not in no Hollywood movies, in these movies by this African American director. Of course, in those days you didn't say no African nothing, you said Negro. But in those Negro movies, though, she wasn't using the name Sweet Marsala; she was calling herself by her own real name.

Anyway, when she first come back to town, a few of us women goes to visit her to tell her how nice she looks. She's our age, but you know how movie stars is; she looks like she 'bout ten, maybe fifteen years younger than us, and reminds me of that woman in the Zora Neale Hurston book about their eyes watching God, when she returns to her town or any of those other colored women on the cinematic screen who looks younger than they actually is.

Cheena say she look 'bout twenty-five years younger than us, and Mishawaka, who's from Mishawaka, Indiana, originally and who people say is part Indian—and yes, we said Indian in those days, not Native American—say she looks thirty-five years younger than us. Mishawaka look at her like she a natural woman, but Cheena, who named after chinaware, looking at her like she think some of her aura of being a movie star might rub off on her. Cheena ain't traveled nowhere; ain't even honeymooned nowhere. But me, I been to Kansas City.

V. Rainbow People

Alexandria.

"They think we're Egyptian," she says, her arm on the divan. "In Ethiopia, they think we're Ethiopian; in Italy, Italians. We've always been sort of rainbow people."

She knows the difference between dadaistic surrealism and fantastic art; sometimes she looks elegant, other times like a worker in the Krupp locomotive factory in Berlin, but always intelligent.

"We were in Ethiopia when the Italians invaded and the Ethiopian war began. Neither the Italians nor the Ethiopians could tell whether we were Italian or Ethiopian. We left Ethiopia and went to Paris and saw Fernandel in 'Le Rosier de Madame Husson,' I believe it was in the Théâtre de la Porte Saint-Martin, I believe it was."

The edge of a window; the sun shines through crystal. A dragon cloud could scrutinize a rainbow.

"A friend of ours came from Germany, a writer, and his family. Non-Aryans, you know."

VI. The Elephant, or Totem and Taboo

Under a strange sky, I wish to be a painter of skies. An anthropologist, a cultural and natural anthropologist, I've been to this country many times in order to study the folklore and the legends of its people. I've written about Mugo wa Kibiru who was said to have prophesied about the coming of the white men. I've written about its women and their occupations and preoccupations. I've written about its animals, especially the *nyoni ya nyagathanga*, that little bird famous for its sweet songs and for, of all the birds, keeping the cleanest and neatest nest. I've written about the *njamba*, its heroes. I've written about the aesthetics and conceptions of beauty here. I've written about its complex music, with its mixture of themes. I've written about its magical narratives.

Many of the people here were surprised to see me, looking just like themselves. When they were told a German woman was coming to the village, they had heard tales of someone called Volkskunde and were not expecting an African German with braided hair. They would not believe that I was from Berlin, and the women did not want me to help them grind corn or gather yams, but I did so anyway.

VII. The Gingerbread Man: An Experiment

He starts playing piano.

Gingerbread Man.

Why do you always call me Gingerbread Man? The Gingerbread Man in the storybook ran. I ain't running.

That's because I'm the Gingerbread Woman. You don't have to run from me.

Why are you looking at me that way?

Because you make me feel marvelous. Why you looking at me that way?

There are unresolved ambiguities in his look that make profound suggestions. He raises up my shirt and kisses my breasts.

John Coltrane.

What?

VIII. Wooley Boatman

We were upstairs in the boardinghouse where she was staying. It was called Wooley Boatman's after the woman who owned it.

"Wooley, this is my cousin Buddy from Kentucky. He's going to be staying with me for a few days. Used to be a soldier."

Wooley looked at me like she hardly believed I was the young woman's cousin, and if I used to be a soldier, then I was the boogie woogie bugle boy.

"None of my business," she said and gave the young woman an extra key.

The young woman's name was Gladys. I had driven to Memphis to see her. I carried my bag up to her room. She'd put a cot in the room along with her bed. When we entered, she glanced at me shyly. I realized just how young she was.

"I had to borrow the cot, but she knows you ain't my cousin, unless it's kissing," she said.

IX. Stephan and Pilar

It was on the island of Madagascar that I was to star in my first movie. I was a girl of seventeen, and it had surprised me that I'd been chosen to play the lead. It was a third world movie in which the players were African Americans, Africans, and Asians. Although people generally called me cute, I was not fair-complexioned, and in those days usually fair-complexioned "colored girls" got the lead. A friend of mine, Alexandria, had convinced me to try out and so I had. Really, though, I'd expected a minor role.

The film is to be made in a mountain village, and so that's where I am, in a long tent where tables have been set up for the players. I'm sitting at one of the tables waiting for the director. Other members of the cast are sitting at the other end of the table, all very garrulous, like they've known each other for years. I suppose many of them have made other movies together. A few of them glance at me out of curiosity, but none comes to join me at my end of the table. This is not only my first movie, but my first trip abroad.

When someone finally comes to my end of the table, they ask me if I'm a friend of Stefan and Pilar.

I say nothing for a moment, and then I say, "My friend Alexandria—I know her well—but I've never met Stefan and Pilar."

X. Mrs. Marsipan

When I first came up North, I was a real shy girl. Mrs. Marsipan had advertised in the "colored notes" of our local newspaper for a Southern girl on account of because she didn't like the behavior of Northern girls, thinking them irresponsible, so I took the train up to Old Saybrook, up in Connecticut. Mrs. Marsipan is what you call one of those eccentric type women and always telling me how she helped to make herself (like you could make yourself with your own hands)—how she helped to make herself, to make and defend herself. And even define herself. And it's all general like that. She don't give no details. And most of the time she comes and tells me that when she sees me on my break reading one of my popular historical novels. (The only real thing I know about her history is that her ancestors are immigrants, but she always refers to them as "settlers," but all working people, you know.) You usually think of settlers as people out West, but her immigrant settlers settled in Old Saybrook and contributed to its growth. (Though from what I see, it ain't grown too far.) Her advertisement tried to attract you to it by making it sound like a real big city.

XI. Aunt Jane's Dream

I had this dream, this weird dream 'bout being an Amazon guide. You say your dream country is Paris, France. Well, mine's for some reason has always been the Amazon. I mean, in this dream I was a real Amazon woman, just like in those *National Geographic* pictures. I might've even had a bone in my bottom lip. I had brown skin and breasts like sweet melons. My hair was black as tar and straight as a spear, and it moved, just like Tina Turner's. Bone in my bottom lip. Girl, it was like wearing earrings. I felt pretty. I had some little scar-like decoration around my breasts, but I didn't get a good look at those, 'cause there was too much going on around me.